The 2023 NORTHWIND *Treasury*

Winners of the Northwind Writing Award

Edited by tara caribou
and Candice Louisa Daquin

Raw Earth Ink

2023

First paperback edition November 2023

Book concept and cover design by tara caribou
Edited by tara caribou & Candice Louisa Daquin

ISBN 978-1-960991-13-3 (paperback)

Published by Raw Earth Ink
PO Box 39332
Ninilchik, Alaska USA 99639
www.raw-earth-ink.com

TABLE OF CONTENTS

ABOUT THE AWARD

The Northwind Writing Award, sponsored by Raw Earth Ink and facilitated by tara caribou, was created to shine light on little known yet exceptional writers across the United States.

The award was granted by process of anonymous scoring by a panel of judges. The judges had no way of knowing who the authors were, so without any bias they were able to score impartially. Overall we looked for writing which stirs emotion, paints vivid imagery, is high-caliber or underappreciated, captures our attention, and lastly, is memorable.

A NOTE FROM THE EDITORS

I love reading and writing. While I am by no means the most accomplished writer myself, I know good writing. I have read enough, and edited enough, that by now I can say this categorically: *Not all writing is equal*. There are outstanding writers who should be recognized. It was for this reason I really relished the opportunity to judge a writing competition.

I like the idea of a competition even as I myself am not competitive. I see it as more than merely *competing*, it is a chance to showcase the best writing submitted and for those who enter, a way to grow as a writer and hone one's craft. Not everyone can win but everyone who enters should feel like a winner for putting their best work out there.

Reading through the submissions was a huge undertaking and incredibly interesting. We all loved the variety of submissions and of course the best part was found in the variety of reading through different genres: fiction, poetry, longer poetry, and non-fiction. Having such a diverse range of writing styles available for the prize, as well as the wide variety of authors in terms of their writing style, made this a fascinating process.

Some of the pieces I read were outstanding. To the point where I was seriously impressed and slightly floored at how well written they were. This motivates me to keep going with the Northwind Writing Award, because it shows a need and a love for writing in our communities.

What was particularly interesting for me personally was how great the non-fiction entries were and many of my fellow judges agreed; I wasn't expecting that. I have unofficially judged writing submissions multiple times in my role as editor with several literary magazines, so it wasn't that different other than the quality of work, which showcased how hard everyone put their best foot forward.

I'm really excited to hold this treasury of that hard work in my hands and see the culmination of all this commitment to the craft of writing. There is no 'one way' of writing well, but there *is* definitely a type of writer who is seriously impressive and can hook you by the first paragraph. This is a collection of those writers. ~Candice Louisa Daquin

When I originally approached Candice with the idea to create an award for exceptional writers across multiple genres, immediately and enthusiastically she was all in. I often come across writers who are of such high caliber and yet don't recognize it for themselves just *how* outstanding they really are. I read. A lot. Much of it, especially in this day of social media and the desire for "everyone to feel like a winner," and with the market so flooded, can be difficult to spot the diamonds in the rough.

I want to showcase those diamonds.

The entries were vast and our judges wonderful. Since I wanted their judging to be completely impartial, no one but I knew who wrote what. I sent out the packets, hundreds of pages each with an alpha-numeric assignment on each entry, to each judge, who also did not know one another. Then came the task of adding up the tallies and comments and notes made by the judges, as well as a couple tie-breaker votes. Once the judging was complete, I read each entry and found myself nearly overwhelmed with excellent writing.

Every one of these winners which you now hold within your hands is to be commended and should be proud of the work they put out.

It has truly been my humble privilege and honor to read their work. I look forward to many more years of treasuries to come. ~tara caribou

OUR JUDGES
Candice Louisa Daquin
Greg Manzi
Lori Felt
Jack "Shorty" Short
Danielle M. Franklin
H. Graham

Tie-breaker/executive scores:
tara caribou

Non-fiction

FROM THE EDITORS: *The juxtaposition of prose-poetry within a non-fiction piece worked incredibly well. There was a dreamlike quality to the telling, exquisite use of language, carefully put together considering the complexity of the story. A true testament to modern times, with unforgettable totems. This is a validation of hard work and spirit, I was deeply moved by the character's experience of education and identity, how she fought for her name, understanding the complexities involved, and the inevitable masking of society, conjured so vividly I felt I was inhabiting the story as a reader. A superb writer. -CLD*

ME LLAMO
by Amanda Trout

A name can be a price.

The Queen of the Moon once desired power, more than what was given to her, more than simple magic and the healing of praying mortals, more than her husband's domain of death or her brother's wars or her sister's rivers. She wanted the sun to fall at her feet, so she molded her magic and sent it slithering into the sun god's realm where it struck his heel and forced its poison deep into his veins, to the very core of his being. When he cried out, she appeared, her scheming self masked by the facade of concerned citizen, master magician, and she begged him for his name—it's the only way she could help, she said, she needed full control, she needed a name far more ancient than that silly sequence of letters gifted by the mortals—and only when the pain threatened to send him into the Duat did the sun god finally pull her close and whisper the sacred syllables into her ear. The weeks that followed saw the Queen place her son on the throne, with the former ruler—foolish, foolish Ra—chained to submission by the mere echo of a word.

Afternoon kindergarten was the worst. The absolute worst, worse than your sisters getting the best snacks or the dog deciding to pee on your bed. You wake up to a rising sun and endless possibilities for play when the clock strikes noon and you're pulled away from it all to sit in a dusty building around people you barely know and don't want to talk to. Your teacher is nice at least. She smiles as she directs all the children into a loose circle. You pretend that smile was meant specifically for you and smile back as you lower yourself to the carpet and fold your hands neatly in your lap. You're the quietest. You want to go first.

"Tell us your name..." the teacher begins. She always starts this way in the early weeks of the school year, the practice as much for her as it is for her students. She fails to see the danger in a ritual almost older than herself, of names given and received in return.

As the years pass by, slow and quick at the same time, the courses get harder and you find out you need glasses, you chop your hair short and hit puberty too fast but the name you exchange always stays consistent. The local Starbucks receives it each time you stop for coffee. You sign it on ballots alongside your partner for the chance at winning a debate. You sell it and your poetry for publication in a magazine.

Two months into your job at the local park you see mysterious dry patches appear on your arms and eyes, bleached white circles of itchy skin that even moisturizer can't seem to cure. It's one of those times where you are two parts curious and three parts afraid. Your dad drives you to the clinic when you're ready to pay $30 to find out what's wrong with you. After the diagnosis (Eczema. Who knew you could actually be allergic to your job?), you drive to the pharmacy and trade your name and $2.50 for a tube of triamcinolone.

————

A name can be a mask.

He claims the name Nobody, wears it like a shield, wields it like the stake he eventually stabs through the giant's eyes. He was Nobody when he clung to the belly of the sheep, Nobody when he poured the giant three goblets of wine, Nobody when doused in cyclop's vomit and the bones of dead men. He was Nobody when the giant cried out to the others of his attempted murder and Nobody still when friends cast the giant's cries aside, for who comes to the aid of the one nobody is hurting? He is Nobody for an instant as he tells his tale to the people of Ithaca, but a mask can never fully fool those who remember the man beneath it, and soon enough he is just Odysseus once more.

The phone rings on Sunday night, evening time, just as you place the last plate down at the dining table filled with your mom's turkey-tomato chili topped with a small pyramid of shredded cheddar cheese. Your mom chastises you for eating too much, especially when you reach for the stack of cornbread muffins and grab two, while she lets the unknown caller ID go to voicemail. The house line is an old white contraption with a miniscule green screen, scarlet-sectioned numbers and a message system that rings out the words as they are being recorded.

"We are calling to talk to Ms. Robi Crusoe..."

Your face goes as red as the phone's blinking numerals. Your mom gives your dad an odd look from across the kitchen.

"Who...?" She barely gets the first word out before you make a small coughing noise and direct all attention on yourself. You've never been good at lying, so why bother.

"Me," you say, and not wanting to explain more, that is where you end. The strange look once on your dad has been turned on you, but you counter it with a pleading look of your own that asks what exactly you need to do now. Your mom lets out a sigh and gestures towards the phone.

"Better call them back." It's the perfect punishment. Your mom knows you too well.

The call goes okay, moreso because you have a name to hide behind and know that they have no chance of finding you. You want to be published some day, but not like this, not when all you have is some voice in a foreign dialect crooning praises to eight-year-old ears, not when you're so insecure about your writing that you can't even claim it as your own.

It takes a long month or two, but the company stops calling you. It takes an even longer ten years, but eventually the pseudonyms stop calling you too.

————

A name can be a key.

In some tales he spins because she asks him to. In others he sneaks into her quarters and spins without permission, straw into gold into misery. In all tales he gives her the choice: deliver to him her firstborn child or say his name. He laughs as she tries vainly, simple titles rolling off her tongue that have no power over him. He's never been Kaspar, Melichor, Skinnyribs or Sheepshanks, nor will he ever be, and he jeers at her before skipping away. The day approaches swiftly and the sprite dances in the open where anyone can witness, the taste of victory honey rushing down his throat and making him drunk. In his stupor he sings an indulgent song laced with the word he's tried so hard to hide. By tomorrow she knows his secret, and all power is no longer his.

Thumb on your buzzer, hands shaking with the weight of a hundred eyes and a thousand expectations, you listen to the reader at the room's front and hope—no, plead—that the question he asks will be something you know.

"But it's not just about knowing," your mental self argues, your over-imaginative mind placing her just out of sight, conjured hand resting on your shoulder. "You've gotta be quicker than everyone else too, and we all know that's not your strong suit."

You don't even know how you got here in the first place, your existence on the school's Scholar's Bowl squad a product of your thirst for knowledge and a chance encounter with a friend-cum-teammate just before you left for work. It didn't take much convincing for you to stay, nor much convincing for your coach to con you and your pride into being an alternate at the first tournament. On second thought, maybe you do know why you're here.

"You're missing all the questions," your self reminds you simply, and you imagine her hand gently nudging your face to the front of the room before settling back, opening your ears to the reader's calm voice.

"What is the title of Leo Tolstoy's debut novel in which a woman commits suicide by throwing her body in front of a train?"

It takes your mind a minute to process fully because it's literature, suicide, Tolstoy, War and Peace, not close enough, the other one, maybe, never read it, what if you're wrong, maybe I'm not, she's the lead, it makes sense, maybe I'm... *Buzz.* Red 3.

"Anna Karenina."

You don't win that round, or the next. Years later you'll win your first medal, third place by a knife's edge. You'll win ten points here and there with your brain. You'll win ten points just because you had to say something. You'll win geeky friends and hour van rides and reasons never to set foot in a Long John Silver's again all because you said a name in a tournament your freshman year, because you said a name that sparked your pursuit of knowledge and power and right.

———

A name is a curse.

Never name a boggart. You may think they're bad at first, filthy little creatures with eyes like congealed blood that prey on your home at night, but these happenings are nothing more than minor pranks compared to the deeds of the named fiend, uncontrollable and unreasonable in its rage against the stranger that bound it to a word.

What follows is a list of your least favorite nicknames:

"Naïve"

"Lazy"

"Ugly"

"Trash"

"Fat"

"Stupid"

"Useless"

And that name a boy called you on the bus in sixth grade that you won't and can't say out loud.

————

A name can be a gift.

There is a practice rooted in ancient Jewish culture that seeks to preserve names in families with a history of early child mortality. The child is not called a true name at birth in fear Death will come for it quickly; it is given the title of "Alterke," Yiddish for "old," in hopes that Death cannot seize a child whose true name isn't known. Only those who survive to the age of marriage are gifted the prize of life, a name, by one of their Patriarchs.

Nights where your sisters actually get along with you remain some of your favorite nights, even when your bouts of playful bickering get a touch out of hand. Tonight was not a night of argument however; the triple chorus of voices spawned from a much more innocent source.

"We're so like the Bears it's not even funny. Just look at Rianne's Ice Bear impression." You turn to your youngest sibling, who has put on her best stoic expression.

"Ice Bear wants lattè" Both twins and you burst into an uncontrollable cackling only quelled by Leah's attempt at continuing your discussion.

"I'm Grizz, obviously." She gestures at herself with a grin before turning her gaze on you. "And you're Panda." Leah frowns when the only reaction she gets from you is a confused look.

"Shouldn't I be Grizz?" you say. "I'm the oldest, he's the oldest, we're both loud and make bad jokes at times; it makes sense."

"But Pan Pan," she whines the name at you and it's like something slides into place in your chest. "You're too much like Panda not to be him, what with the geekiness and the awkwardness and the..."

"You can stop now," you chide in the lovingly annoyed way all older sisters master from the womb. "I get it. And that works for me."

"YAY!"

Later that week the nickname slips out of your mouth, then your parents. Eventually it's a term of endearment, a pun on your name, a piece of your childhood you never want to let go.

You secretly hope your sisters never let it go either.

————

A name can be a choice.

Fiction tells of a girl who made her life selling words, phrases and speeches that sparked emotions in the people of her world. It was only natural that she would sell a pair of words to herself: the name "Belisa," meaning "slender one," the name "Crepusculario" meaning "twilight." And this is ultimately what she becomes, a woman who sees herself how she wants to be seen, who slips away from trouble like twilight slips to dark, who saves the broken life of a coronel with time, a whisper and just two words.

Sitting at a pressed wood table at the front of room 101, you draw the laminated sheet towards you and, running the tip of your finger across its pristine smoothness, you begin to decide what name you will hold for the rest of the year.

It's a tradition in your high school's Spanish classes: each student casts off their past in favor of their future by taking on a name befitting their first foray into a new culture. You know this choice is important. The name must be something you would willingly be called, something that rolls off the tongue, something with some *meaning* to it.

Then you see it, a name both similar to your own yet unique, a combo of rich vowels and strong consonants. You whisper it under your breath and it's like your heart pounds with the syllables. It's different from anything your classmates have picked, and this is what makes it perfect.

When your teacher calls your name you stand and lightly push your chair in. You turn to face her and firmly state the name you choose. Later, when the rest of the students stand as well to begin practicing introductions, you face the friend to your right and own your new name with a smile on your face.

"Hola, me llamo Marta. ¿Y tú?"

FROM THE EDITORS: *On a personal level this spoke to me, I think even if it hadn't I would have valued the solid structure of this story and its ultimate message. Most of us have experienced something akin to this in our lives, the idea of being able to go back and thank someone who shaped our lives, even as they didn't know it. Rendered very well through a slow burn development of character and story, despite being a short-story, is hard to get 'right' and this hit the mark and then some. -CLD*

BASKING
by Angela Townsend

If the Walrus Guy knew, he never said anything to shame me. But the Walrus Guy knew.

Managing a dining hall is difficult business for any mammal. Throw in a shoreline of militant vegans and earnests metaphysically opposed to paper towels, and you had best enlist the angels. I was as meatless as most Vassar freshmen, but I intended no tsunamis. It would be enough if I could be the new moon, out of the lens and in my own secret talks with the tide.

My secret made love to the spotlight, my driftwood arms offering tell-alls for no pay. I had packed "eating issues" between my Bible and my daisy sweater, though I blamed them on my diabetes and my homesickness. An ill-advised pixie cut made me look like a Dum-Dum lollipop, but my hair refused to grow back. When new friends made puns and proclamations about my single apple or 36-ounce Diet Coke for breakfast, I started going to the dining hall alone.

There was no way to go it alone at 6am, the hour when "ACDC" – the All-Campus Dining Center – teemed with life. Gathering strength to save the world, my sleeping classmates missed the carnival.

There was the Java City man, swinging carafes like kettlebells to the rhythm of freestyle: "Ain't no city like a Java City, 'cause a Java City got style!"

There was the omelet dowager, all perfect posture over her wok, studying me like a mutant squid.

There was the apologetic professor, spilling Chex and declaring herself "a bit of a wonderland today."

There was the Walrus Guy, roaring mightily over them all.

He noticed me first, antennae buzzing by October. "Well good morning, young lady!" His mustache moved like an independent entity. "You're our first lark of the day. It's a gift to love the morning."

He saw me choose my apples as carefully as sand dollars, two for breakfast and three to stretch across the day. "Do you like those little McIntosh? I could see about getting some other varieties."

He respected my Diet Coke consumption. "Coffee isn't for everyone. Options are wonderful."

He talked about his daughters, which made me tell him that I was a daughter.

"My youngest loves fruit like you," he said, wielding Cream of Wheat packets. "She's at Northwestern."

"Illinois, right?"

"Too far for my liking."

"You're close."

"Extremely. She's my pearl. Gonna be an honest journalist. Where's your family?"

"Just an hour away," I admitted, "but I'm a terrible baby. I go home most weekends. My Mom is my best friend."

Why was I telling him this?

"Young lady, that's a gift few receive." He was half-grandfather, half-Lorax, suspended fully in the moment. "You enjoy that bond."

It was safer to talk about majors than cottage cheese, but one door opened another. "I thought I would be an English major, but Anthropology is calling my name." I pulsed the crushed ice.

"Headed for Papua New Guinea?"

I laughed. "I'm too homesick to go to New Jersey. But I never knew Anthro is a way of looking at the world, a lens. It takes the human story seriously. It's all about asking people questions and caring about the answer."

"You could take that anywhere."

"Right. If you love people, Anthro fits."

"It sounds like a good fit for you, young lady."

He said this even though he always saw me alone, the first seal on the beach of morning. Shameless carbonation and fat apples on my tray, I would bask in the window, watching Vassar resurrect. I sliced my McIntoshes – and then gaudy Golden Deliciouses and luxury Honeycrisps – into cubes as small as snails. I played with my bendy-straw and wrote questions in my notebook.

I sang to the Java City man. "Ain't no city like a Java City, 'cause a Java City's got ME!"

"Lookin' pretty in the city!" he whooped.

I asked the omelet woman how long she'd worked at Vassar. "Thirty years, my dear. Scary to think how many eggs we've cracked in that time."

I picked up the wonderland's stash of Sweet n' Lows. "The secret of my success!" It turned out she was a religion professor with a sweet spot for the Gospel of Thomas.

Just after Christmas, my sea-captain mother cornered me onto a counselor's couch, and I agreed to eat a little more protein.

"But I won't eat eggs." I dropped anchor. "I can't touch peanut butter. I don't know what to do."

"Can you talk to the dining hall people?" My mother has always commanded waves easily.

"I can do that." I surprised myself.

I did not surprise the Walrus Guy. "Oh, most certainly!" He seemed relieved the day I asked about cottage cheese. "Do you have a preferred brand? Let's see what we can do."

The next day, he was waiting by the Northern magnolia in front of ACDC. "Young lady, step this way."

We descended into the bowels of the dining hall, a buzzing berth I had never imagined. The industrial fridge was a frigate, an aircraft carrier for plant-based milks and Lactaids and...

"...these are yours." The Walrus Guy lifted a tub of Daisy in each hand. "I won't put them out there where someone else may take a scoop. You have my blessing to come down and get what you need. I'll make sure we always have these for you."

"I don't want you to go to all that trouble—"

"—it's no trouble. You just promise me that if there's ever any problem, you'll let me know right away. Okay?"

"Okay."

It turns out protein is no small thing. My hair started growing in a patchy reef of hope. I joined the Taizé fellowship and sang French hymns by night. My advisor helped me secure an internship at an Oldies radio station.

"The anthropology of the Beach Boys!" The Walrus Guy exulted. "Who knew?"

"I'm going to study the bond between listeners and voices," I bubbled. "People form relationships with deejays without ever seeing their faces. Why is that?"

"Why is that?" his whiskers exulted. "An excellent question!"

But this meant I would have to catch a cab at 4am, with ACDC's doors still locked. "Are you here in the afternoons?"

"Afraid not, young lady. But you know where to find everything you need."

I certainly did not. But I knew where to find the cottage cheese, and the new Pink Lady apples (who knew?), and the coffee that suited me fine when anointed with five Sweet n' Lows.

In all our conversations, I never learned the Walrus Guy's name, and he never asked mine. He was grace in maroon flannel, the first handlebars to steady my vessel. Twenty years later, on the coast of forty, I had one more answer for him.

I had determined to celebrate my frightening birthday by writing forty letters of gratitude. I trawled my timeline with a metal detector, pulling silver from every decade. There was never any question that the Walrus Guy would make the list.

But how does one send a letter to "Mustache of Mercy, c/o ACDC"? Surely, he had long since roared his last on Vassar's shores, those talkative tusks enjoying retirement.

Still, I had to try. "The man who ran the dining hall in 1999 was a beacon of compassion," I understated the case to Human Resources. "He had a voluminous mustache and a huge heart. Is there any chance you could send him my letter?"

"That's Roy." No investigation was necessary.

"Tell me he's still alive."

"Very much so. Still lives in Poughkeepsie. Send your letter."

Language was too shallow for all I wanted to say, but I splashed about as best I could. He had made me feel like a pearl right there in my grief and goo. He had asked seagulls to sing when I'd only heard shrieking.

He had commanded cottage cheese and safety, and one bony freshman would go on to trust that "home" happens on many shores.

He never wrote back, but perhaps that's best. Our friendship was never about answers. The Walrus Guy may not remember me, but I can't forget the time before I felt safe. Roy may never know the power of his roar, but he knew what he knew.

FROM THE EDITORS: *Whilst sad stories can be incredibly hard to read, this was irresistible. Much like FireFly Lane this reads as a realistic memorial to love between friends. At times the cruelty of the perspective was shocking and a reminder of how humans are in their secret hearts, unable to cope with death and dying, and have ugly thoughts about those they love. Other times the revealed depth of love was breathtaking. I was moved to tears which is unusual. An incredibly powerful piece of writing. My favorite was the lists; such an innocuous human thing I felt it was done exquisitely and with deep sensitivity to something we all feel at some point in our lives. A real testament to life and death. -CLD*

MEMENTO: A NONFICTION SEQUENCE
by Kathryn O'Day

"I'm me, again," you said that April afternoon, clicking your compact shut.

And in that moment, you *were* you – the you before cancer, I mean. Only now so tiny, bones poking as you lit your cigarette.

"I should have been at the opening last night," you sighed, exhaling. "But I was so tired."

"Are you sure you're up for it, now?" I asked. "I can walk Boris while you rest."

"No, I can do it. I just have to keep this with me" –*this* being a brick-sized purse and a tube that snaked up your shirt –"chemo-to-go," you called it as you fished some plastic bags and a leash from a pile near the door, then handed them to me. I did my best to steady the overjoyed Boris, who bounded out the door to the gate as we picked our way around the dog droppings and random tools (including, disturbingly, a rotating saw) that littered your front yard.

The café was only two blocks away, but you moved slowly, careful not to trip on uneven planes of Chicago sidewalk and resting every hundred feet or so. I hovered, doing my best to match your pace without letting go of the leash whenever Boris lunged at a passer-by.

"I can't believe I sold my café to a bunch of Jesus-lovers," you grumbled, then launched into your favorite fable about a woman you met who "didn't mind" caring for her dying father because doing so would "get her into Heaven" – you paused to stamp out your stub and drop it in a bin outside the unisex on the corner "—These *people*," you muttered.

Crabby-you vanished, though, by the time we arrived at the café, replaced by that gracious lady who once chatted with regulars and plied their children with treats. "I'm sorry I missed the opening," you purred. "I just wanted to wish you good luck."

"That's very thoughtful of you," the new Christian café-owner said.

But she didn't offer you a seat.

We turned and headed back. Slower, now, with more stops.

Two months later, I gave you a pitcher shaped like a fish for your birthday.

A month after that, you were dead.

———

I was in the kitchen, packing lunches, when our friend, Laura, called with the news. As if you didn't have enough drama: dog, café, ex-husband.

And now cancer. Stage Four. Colon, lungs, liver.

It hadn't been good between us for a while. You'd grown flaky with age, making plans and never showing up. You'd grown flaky, and I'd grown impatient. "Could you, maybe, *call* when you're not coming?" I'd asked (and yes, it was on your birthday).

"You're so judgmental!" you screamed, then flounced out of the bar.

Which is true. I *am* judgmental.

Still, that doesn't make me wrong.

Now, though, you were dying. It was all over Google: "End of life." "Late stage." "Final days." "Death."

What can a friend do? I typed.

"Reach out," Google replied. So, I called you and invited myself over.

———

Your place was even worse than usual —random bits of foam ripped from the couch, sticky wads of crumbs and hair, yogurt containers furred with mold.

"I'll tidy," I said, looking for a sponge.

There was exactly one in your kitchen.

I scrubbed your gummy dishes with it. I emptied the ashtrays, tossed the yogurt. I wiped down the surfaces and swept the floor and listened to your complaints. You complained about your sister, who cried too much. You complained about the doctor, who expressed no emotion at all. You complained about your employees who whined about extra shifts. I shook my head, saying they took advantage of you.

I can't deny that a part of me wondered whether you were exploiting your newfound misery. You'd always been a prolific moaner, especially in the years since your divorce, sighing massive sighs about your former friend who sided with your ex, your former landlady who was suing you for back rent, your former dentist to whom you would never give another dime, your neighbor's former boyfriend who took the front stairs when Boris was in the yard. These *people*, you'd lament.

Forgive me, Sarah. I didn't yet know about the slow poison of chemo-to-go.

And even if I did, I couldn't allow the fact of your suffering to enter my busy, busy brain or the cage that holds my heart.

———

You called a few days later.

"How dare you make me feel bad about my employees!" you screamed into the phone.

"I was trying to be supportive," I said.

"How can you be supportive when you're so judgmental?" you squawked.

How can I be supportive when you're so batshit crazy? I thought.

I didn't say that, though, because I'd consulted Google again for tips on being a good friend to someone with cancer. "None of this is about you," Google told me.

So, I didn't tell you that you were batshit crazy (even though you were). Instead, I said:

"Sarah, I'm sorry that things are hard. I understand if you need some time apart. Just remember, you can call me anytime."

I hung up, feeling virtuous, and folded the rest of the laundry.

I understand. That's what a good friend would say. I was a good friend, the kind of friend who would forgive you for yelling at her after she hired a babysitter so that she could scrub your sticky dishes with a smelly old sponge.

You never did call back, though.

And we didn't talk for a full year.

———

Here are some things I did that year, according to my phone:

1) I cut my hair short to save time in the morning.
2) I dressed my daughter in a fluffy pink dress and a homemade crown for her fifth birthday.
3) I ate deep-fried butter with my family at the Indiana state fair.
4) I composed numerous learning objectives and wrote them on the whiteboard for my high schoolers to ignore.
5) I chaperoned a group of students on a college tour.
6) I celebrated as my Academic Decathlon team won fourth place in the city.
7) I cut felt and glued craft foam for my children's Halloween costumes.

Here are some things I did according to memory:

1) Drink
2) Cry

Until your sister called to tell me I'd better reach out or I might never talk to you again.

———

"I want to reach out," I said. "But Sarah's still mad at me."

"All you have to do is apologize," your sister said.

"For what?" I asked. *For deserting my family to clean your house? For listening? For "understanding?"*

"Just say you're sorry," she said. "I'm sure she'll forgive you."

I wasn't sorry, but we hadn't talked for an entire year.

"How have you been?" I texted that night.

This provoked one of your rants about how judgmental I was and how I always made you feel worse when people were mean to you, and did I know, by the way, that you were dying of cancer? Did I know that? How I had betrayed you, and how you didn't need people like me in your life, people who acted as if you were already dead, cleaning up your house and throwing away all your things. "I'M NOT DEAD YET!" you texted.

"I'm sorry," I texted back. (Even though I still thought you were batshit crazy – even more so, possibly. I wasn't sorry; I was humoring you because of the cancer, not because you were right. I was humoring you because it didn't even matter, because you may not be dead now, but you would be soon, and we both knew it. I was humoring you because I couldn't take your silence anymore, because I was terrified that you'd die and haunt me forever.)

I'm sorry, I texted, just please talk to me, Sarah, I'm so sorry, and please forgive me, Sarah, I love you so much and I miss you so much and I so want to be there for you and please, please forgive me, Sarah.

I stared at the screen.

Finally you texted back. I was welcome to come visit on Sunday, if I liked.

————

And when Sunday finally came it was almost like the way it was long ago between us, before cancer, before all your feuds, before you caught your husband cheating –the way it was that summer I bartended to pay my way through school and we spent all night drinking whiskey from a gallon jug on my stoop.

Only now you were so tiny –opening your mouth like a baby bird for the bit of pastry I brought along.

"Thanks for bringing Napoleons," you said, and then you let me wash the dishes with your smelly old sponge.

————

Looking back on those last four months, these are the things I remember:

    1) Stepping over the rotating saw on my way out (Why did the workmen leave it in your front yard amidst the dog-droppings? Why did you choose to renovate your kitchen when you knew you were dying?)

    2) Watching you scarf down a cream-filled "cronut" and half of a box of peppermint patties after we smoked weed to stimulate your appetite.

    3) Gripping the leash whenever I took Boris for a walk.

    4) Your face that time you talked about death. We were crouched side by side in the only nook that wasn't covered in sawdust in between the kitchen and the front room of your house. You were smoking (of course you were.) I want to say we were drinking something –probably coffee. You looked over at me, your eyes soft and wondering and wise and resigned. "I'm not afraid of being dead," you said. "I'm just afraid of dying."

    5) Your birthday party. You opened presents, then immediately went to bed. Silently we tidied (there were six of us, I want to say), then left you to rest.

Tiny farewells, all of them. Like those knocks at the door when my daughter would slip out of her bunk for one last kiss goodnight.

————

I had just arrived in St. Louis for a weekend road trip when Laura called again, crying.

"You'd better come back," she said.

So, I did. I gassed up, turned around, and drove five and a half hours back to Chicago, catching you just before they wheeled you in to Intensive Care. I waited around with everyone else (your birthday party, reunited), but then gave up and headed home, pretty sure you'd be dead when I awoke.

————

How strange to find you sitting up in bed the next morning, your sister smiling by your side. "I'm going home," you announced.

"She's going home!"

I kept repeating it as everyone else trickled in, red-eyed from the night before. "She's going home!" I'd say brightly, even though I wasn't sure what exactly "going home" meant.

Jenny didn't, either, and burst into tears when I told her. The others laughed then, reassuring her that you weren't "going home to Jesus." I laughed, too, pretending I'd known all along that you were going home to die.

Your sister took over then, assigning tasks. Call the loved ones. Clean the apartment (the kitchen was ready, thank God, although it was still covered in sawdust). Tend to the dog. Greet the guests. By the end of the day, the hospital room was packed with them.

"I want to hear some jokes!" you demanded, and obediently we took turns sharing our favorites. Mine: what did the mayonnaise say to the refrigerator?

Close the door —I'm dressing!

You and your sister sang a song you had once sung when you were children. The rest of us listened and laughed, perched at the window, leaning in the doorway, crouched against the wall, as the room grew golden in the light of the setting sun.

———

A day later, they wheeled you back home. I'd cleared the space with Jenny, who had thoughtfully packed aprons and two cans of Pledge.

I brought sponges.

We were all waiting for you when the ambulance arrived. Laura did her best to restrain Boris, but he broke free, anyway, and bounded all over you. (He's in Los Angeles now, bounding all over your sister, probably.)

"You know what I want," you murmured, touching my arm.

"No, what?" I asked.

"A cigarette and a glass of wine," you said.

I knew you couldn't take much more than a puff and a sip, but I brought them anyway. "I have to go," I mumbled, then rushed out to catch a ride home with Jenny. Both of us were late picking up our kids from camp.

———

I hated your memorial service. At the time, I told myself it was because of the MC and his phony, theatrical mannerisms. Who *was* this person, anyway? You'd never introduced us or even talked about him. Why did *he* get to narrate the slideshow of your life, pictures I had never seen? And then I thought something very unkind: that the over-the-top Sarah in the slideshow was the Sarah you pretended to be when you dropped in on the Christian café-owner. Gracious lady Sarah, not the Sarah who grumbled.

I've clung to that thought for years, probably because I don't like the truth: that the real reason I hated that memorial service was because I saw so little of myself reflected there. As if we were not dear, dear friends. As if I were insignificant.

Was I?

If I were to ask Google, it would tell me that your death, like your cancer, is not about me. If I were to ask Google, it would tell me that this is your story, not mine.

But Google doesn't know either of us.

So maybe it should butt out.

In June, just before you died, I gave you a pitcher shaped like a fish for your birthday. A few months later, your sister gave it back to me. It is my one memento of you, my dear, dear, friend. That and a photo of the two us with Laura and Jenny smiling at the lake.

EVERYONE MELTS
by Kaci Skiles Laws

I knew my grandpa for six short years. I remember the indention where he sat on his side of the bed, hours of each day as he aged, his slippers sliding over the yellow linoleum into the kitchen for more coffee, his inquisitive face as he listened to Trade Fair on his small radio with the dials that if he turned too much would create a hiss of static before they fell off and rolled under the stove or fridge and he'd shout some profanity, the chair he died in.

———

My first memory of him was smiling while I was crying. He held out a spoon with something cold on the end. "Ice cream solves everything." He said. I swallowed and said, "Bite," opening my mouth like a baby bird a dozen times. It was my second word.

Every summer after I'd carry a wafer cone full of chocolate ice cream, always chocolate, as if it were an extension of me. I missed him, and in her own way my grandma did too, so I was allowed an endless amount because grief makes people melt. It runs down their cheeks, and they don't talk as much. I could ask for anything, and the answer was *yes*. The answer was, *please be happy* and obvious: *ice cream*. We carried on that way. As a child my grandparents' house was a gray safe haven with a few monsters tucked in places.

———

"Listen, if you're ever playing hide and seek," my dad would look at my sisters and I, loud, his face long, "Don't go getting into any of those refrigerators in the shed. You won't be able to open the door from the inside if you do. No one will know you're in there, if we can't find you..."

It reminded me of the poor bride that died hiding in an old trunk on her wedding day. It was just a game. It was supposed to be fun. It wouldn't open once it was shut.

The shed smelled like antifreeze, and the closest I ever got was just a peek.

He didn't have to warn me about the thing in the red barn. I'd unlatched and opened the door enough times to let the rush of musty wood invade my nose and long enough to let light in. The shadows at the back were black and long holding a circular saw. It felt ominous to me, like the spinning wheel in Sleeping Beauty, with its rusty, hungry teeth. I wondered when the last time it had eaten. It was my grandpa's, and his hands had not touched it ever in those six years or after. He was busy putting his hands on other things. I learned about the other things later, fragments, from listening to the grown-ups talking, and one day when I was thirty my dad sat me down and said,

"He tried to kill Mama once. I had my pistol pointed at him, and I almost..."

All I could see was the pistol in my dad's hand when I was ten by the screen door, his eye aiming, and the snake raising its head out of the grass by the side of the house. The copperhead exploded, and it was the Fourth of July in spring.

I saw red. I heard the bullet break the sound barrier, and the snake's body was sacred geometry spinning in the dirt. My grandpa never knew what a great shot my dad was.

———

Another time, before the Vietnam War, my grandpa was different. He tried to save a girl in the same spot he'd almost killed my grandma. The evidence was tucked under the sheets. My grandma had them pinned into the mattress. I had to be careful if I wanted to see the stains or else get stuck. One day my grandma asked me what I was doing, and I asked for ice cream.

There were two stories, and in the first one the girl lived, the ambulance was quick, her neck was mended. It was—*a terrible accident.* In the real version, a young boy and girl came around a ninety degree corner too quick. The motorcycle was mangled, and there were bodies; my grandparents' fence was like a web. There must have been screaming and crunching and silence before the porch light illuminated the yard. My dad never did tell me because he couldn't recreate any of the sounds, as a boy of twelve it was all pictures flashing, ringing, snow, cold.

The boy got up and the bloody girl didn't. *The bloody girl.* My grandpa carried her by the legs and told the boy to keep her head still as my grandma held the door to the house and made way to their bedroom. My dad stood by the door frame of his room and saw the linoleum spotted with dark drips after they passed. My grandma ran back by his door, red soaked into her robe, reaching for the phone. He counted three clicks on the rotary phone. He counted three clicks as the gurney touched down outside, was raised and rushed over the wooden porch. Voices and the last click of it sliding back inside the ambulance, the red lights off, the siren quiet.

I would ask him if he ate ice cream after, but I knew it was too cold that night. I'd like to think there were cookies and warm milk. I imagined a fire. My dad caught my grandpa's eye as he walked behind my grandma and a trail of sheets and blankets. He kept walking, and my dad closed his door until morning.

———

The morning after my grandpa died I had to tell my teacher I wouldn't be in class. I was six and crying; she didn't offer me a spoon with something cold on the end. She smiled and said, *okay.* I felt out of place. I had to stay when all I wanted was to go home. I thought about ice cream and chewed the eraser off the end of my pencil.

At his funeral I heard my cousin say, *Look, she doesn't understand.* I was angry because I did. He looked smooth and gray in his casket like a baby in its mother's womb. I ran a thumb across his cheek when no one was looking. I was thinking about how much I hated crying in front of people, how cold his skin felt, so I had to pee a lot.' Everyone melts differently.

———

It was the last secret that melted me the most. My dad didn't talk to my grandpa for years after he almost killed him. Many nights leading up to that moment my grandpa would sit as a silhouette in his pick-up surrounded by smoke. The pasture by the house would wait, and he'd be grateful for it and the pink sky, his Marlboros' bright fire ends as he took each drag and his sipping whiskey in which he swallowed like soda pop wanting it to solve everything because ice cream stopped working somewhere along the way. His revolver rested in the passenger seat always, as if for company, comfort. It never did get him, but his cancer did. It made him the most angry he'd ever been, but he never could pull the trigger because behind it all he was really just melting.

MY ARRANGED MARRIAGE
by Tulip Chowdhury

A big part of my teenage years was spent in Europe with my parents and brother in the late 60's. The Western culture shaped my romantic notions, which differed from my Bangladeshi Muslim family heritage. I was twenty-one years old by the late 70s and was waiting for my prince charming to sweep me off my feet and let people say what they wanted. Alas! My youthful dreams of finding love, being kissed under the moonlight, and having a love-filled married life evaporated when my guardians arranged my marriage.

I had an enlightened family and did not wish to force me into a marriage. The Bangladeshi society of the late 70s stood firm for arranged marriages for young men and women. A good upbringing reflected on not falling in love or waiting patiently for the guardians to decide who a suitable life partner could be. And that was my hesitancy to find my prince. How could I hurt my family? I was an avid reader from an early age. Reading about romance got me to weaving dreams of being in the arms of a young man who will whisper, "I love you." Though falling in love in those days was considered a social disgrace for girls with good upbringings, I would imagine a knight rescuing me from what I thought was a "social malady" in which marriageable girls did not look for life partners for themselves. However, my father was romantic beyond his time. I grew up watching my father bring flowers and gifts for my mother that would light up her face. Like my parents, I hoped I would find romance somewhere, even in an arranged marriage.

My family was back in Bangladesh when my wedding bells rang. I met my husband on my bridal bed. Since my prince charming did not come to kiss me under the moonlight, I dreamed my husband would be the love of my life. On the night of my wedding, as customary, in my bridal outfit, I waited on the decorated bed. My husband, dressed in his marriage outfit, came to join me. I was scared, for I had never been so close to an unknown man. But I knew better than to resist him as he lifted the long veil that covered my head. That was like a beginning to show his rights as a husband, to dare to unveil me. My husband took my hand and told me about my duties to the in-laws. I was the family's eldest son's wife, the "Boro Bou," which also meant caring for his younger siblings. I listened and touched his feet to seek blessing from the man there to care for me.

I held my breath as he put out the lights. Indeed, what was to come? The physical bonding would have some elements of romance, a unique touch as I had heard my friends speak of. Sigh! There was nothing to make me memorable for the day, no rings or flowers to say that we had a connection beyond the arranged circumstances of our lives. The first night of marriage came and went, virginity lost and innocent dreams too. Romance in marriage rested like a pearl in its shell of dreams, nurtured by endless hopes. Deep inside, though, I realized I was against a big challenge in life.

My colorful notions of a romantic relationship with my husband got wrapped in the deluge of family life as days became whirlwinds of cooking, raising family, and social obligations took me to shore to shore. It was a marriage of convenience, and being the eldest brother's wife among ten siblings, I had a significant role to play. The years were like double-edged swords with solid family elements, yet the heart flew to distant lands. Broken dreams of love walked on sand, steps that threatened to give away and make me fall. Luckily, I did not stumble and fall, no matter how challenging life seemed. When my first baby, a son, arrived, there was much more to look forward to than a romantic life partner. Roller coaster life began with my first taste of motherhood, looking after my brothers and sisters-in-law living with me.

My husband and I were two different people. Growing up in the village in a conservative family, he had minimal idea of arts and culture. But to me, filling my aesthetic senses was very important, at times above other things. I often skipped meals to finish a good book or spent hours under a full moon star gazing. I bought books or watercolors with the money I was supposed to pay for my medicines. I could not pursue my husband to share time doing something to lift the heart out of the struggle of the daily routine.

On the other hand, I could not join his thoughts on politics or sports. An incomplete puzzle followed me in the emptiness of our married life. I soon understood that love could not be coerced in anyone's heart. Neither of us would fall in love, but may we learn to care and respect each other. It was a marriage of convenience. He was a dutiful husband, which was suitable for a life partner. A wise woman made her marriage work; I was expected to make the best of what I had. Divorces were shunned in our times then. I sometimes felt like running away, but I could not escape my family values. At times, I remembered a distant cousin who eloped with the love of her life, one who was not to be mentioned in family gatherings. I wondered if she was happy. Happiness then sang and danced on the other side of the field. I would stop stirring my fish dish on the stove and get lost in my thoughts. Do choices, fate, and happiness march together?

As married life progressed, I felt as if there was a wall between my husband and me. My dreams of a love life had a rude awakening to a man. Since romance was missing from the first day of the marriage, I took to more of doing things after my heart. But I missed sharing the "us" time. I did not feel like a loved wife sharing a life, more like a helper in his life with our own in the package. I went for a teaching job to help with the finances after the birth of my third child. Marriages are supposed to be made in heaven. I decided that the invisible forces of heaven had my Mills and Boon hero lost their ways. We shared no candlelit dinners or had a honeymoon. My beloved reading, music, and art became my battles. He disliked books in the bedroom, and I couldn't sleep without bedtime reading. I loved music, and he thought it distracted me from my wifely duties, a notion from his village upbringing, a society where wives focused only on the household.

My husband was a good provider, though he was in no way the lover or companion my heart longed for. Living married was like dispersing my duties to the social norms. In those times of a male-dominated society, a man was satisfied as long as the stove was running and the family was doing well. Amid it all, the wife was the doer, with hardly anyone to attend to her. Sometimes, I would cook something special and wait for my husband to say a good word about it or to thank me. But none came. All seemed to be considered a signed agreement without any need for appreciation. To the outsider, we were the perfect couple. However, my inner being asked every sunrise, *What kind of a life was my empty marriage?* Though shadows of our differences kept our hearts far apart, the children, two boys, and one girl, were like bridges, allowing life to flow between us. We shared the roof but hardly knew each other.

Our disparity hung heavy in the air. I never understood why my husband repeatedly watched the local news on six channels. He did not know why I wanted him to walk with me when spring was smiling with all her colors on nature. He wondered how I could spend the whole afternoon buried in a book. My father-in-law had forbidden me to sing, and so I took refuge in listening to music. But I could not do so when my husband was home. He disliked my music and hated the books I kept in my room. And I was not too fond of the beetle- -nuts he chewed like gums when he was home. But my dreams of romance still hung by threads through novels by Nicholas Sparks and Danielle Steel. He often said those books were for teenagers, not a mother of three. Over time, we grew used to each other strangely, both set in continuous adjustments to daily life. We mewed and barked like Tom and Jerry but continued our family. I returned to my reading and writing to keep my aesthetic self alive.

But somewhere deep, the perennial flower, the flower *Tulip* inside me, refused to be crushed and kept coming to life with the warmth of my name. With my marriage, I accepted that oil and water do not mix and that my husband would not blend in hearts. Despite our differences, we raised three wonderful children who eventually moved to the USA. My arranged marriage was my fate; my takeaway is my children. I also realized a man who could not reach my heart with his set ways was a wonderful father up and beyond. Marriages seemed to be tests of patience and adjustments, tests that keep us on the alert all the time.

Friends' marriages built on exciting romance crumble from time to time. I wonder how my one survived for over three decades, minus the ingredient of romance. Perhaps my no-romantic marriage was a double-edged sword that allowed me to have a family of children who love me unconditionally. Love in all aspects comes in strange ways, as did for me. We cannot have things perfect in life, and the absence of romance in married life was one missing thing. God has blessed me with children and a hundred other ways, and I am now happy to let go of my romantic dreams. I am pretty sure that my husband was not in the marriage either. To him, I was not what he would have wished to have for a wife. But pushing aside our differences, we built a family, which is our success in contributing to the continuation of the human race.

Prose Poetry

FROM THE EDITORS: *When a piece of writing literally blows you back into your seat and you need to stop and collect yourself, when you find yourself saying out-loud, "wow, wow, so true"... you know you've read something special & utterly unique. The vivid imagery whisks me along and I am bound to ride it until the end. -TC*

ECHOES OF STALE AIR
by Braeden Michaels

I feel like a scattered deck of cards, an ace of trembles, queen of teardrops, and the lost signature of spades. I have a name that can't be forgotten but my personality feels slightly dim. I am a 1969 penny without any shine, Abraham Lincoln is slightly faded. Astrology is just a stack of stars you can barely see in a fog. I have a tattoo of my sign laughing at the face of death. Buckle up, people treat me like a railroad track and never glancing at the scenery. I am a dog-hungry artist that gets lost in the canvas. You can feel my tribulations in the colors. My past is full of decorated tragedies and continues to clean my mouth out with a cup of cynicism daily.

I feel like a tumultuous storm, a cyclone without direction. Parts of me are shades of havoc and parts of me only have splinters of peace. I feel like an oxymoron with riddles prancing in my awakened mind. Yes, I am a chatterbox around my two-millimeter circle of friends. I am quiet around those who want to box me up and place every label on me, then place me in a warehouse of Amazon. Yes, I am slightly scatterbrained, and my routine has the vanilla taste. I've only contemplated suicide once, intoxicated and numb simultaneously. The morning arrived and knew I didn't have the guts. I knew everyone would identify me as weak and a coward. Yellow is not my skin color.

I feel like a soul that has stared into blisters behind a barbaric cage and has never seen a flower bloom. I have never seen a shimmering rainbow or the wings of a butterfly. I feel like a never-ending catastrophe without any armor. My strength is buried behind all the obligations and the fake smile. The quiet melody playing between my ears brings me peace. I embrace the harmony and lyrics of simplicity to remove the complexity within the chaos. I feel like I have remains of myself floating around my sinful body. I feel as if I am constantly swimming, and my head is barely above a tidal wave. I am barely breathing. I am living but don't feel alive.

I feel like a pocket of a pair of pants owned by a homeless man. I'm a breath of stale air. Nothing about me is compelling. Just ask my backbreaking lover, who continually insults my intelligence as I shed my layers. I've learned to build my walls with pillars, not bricks. I've learned to hide my natural instincts and my spirituality that has slowly corroded. Something about me is disappearing and struggling to see the ray of hope. I've learned to camouflage the anger for my children. I love all of them with the discomfort in my heart. I feel like a piece of paper from a diary and the words seem to echo.

FROM THE EDITORS: *To allow a poem to take on a life and a personality on its own, to birth it, give it wings, and release it to become as it will, all without losing control is a feat rare to behold.-TC*

ARS POETICA – THE SKIN OF THIS POEM
by Rachael Ikins

The skin of this poem is soft, wind-washed soft like when you rub the back of your hand over your own cheek. You bend to paint flower boxes to match the barn, your flying hair sticks to the wetness. A pair of vultures floats overhead. Without moving they drift, a Celtic knot of Spring gratitude for winter's roadkill.

A poem is a kicked ant hill. You didn't mean to step on their stone's lid—a sudden froth of activity, workers, others carrying eggs in their mandibles, wincing in brash sunlight they flow. Someone must remember to bring the queen.

Scylla's carpet spreads bluer under daffodil's heavy heads, fragrance evokes your mother; Bermuda shorts, worn denim jacket. She leans on her dandelion sticker. Lover of vegetables, she had no idea the nutrients—iron, vitamins B and C, contained in their stubborn stains. Dandelion-flower cookies, dandelion syrup, you create all these, sweetness that never crossed your mother's plate.

You wonder, her alcoholism a species of sugar addiction. While you giggle dizzy after just a teaspoon of wine, you find yourself back and back to the pantry for another chocolate egg, another jellybean one more sweet and high.

Poetry is a sugar rush, licking your lips, your fingers, as a thrush calls from woods' edge. Those warbled notes crack your heart's shell every April. Words hatch, "a fairy! it is magic!"

You run outside unable to breathe indoors. With only sky above, your heart slows. You follow the path to the pond, the road home at sunset; remove your shirt, your pants, a cast-off skin.

And while tongues of grass taste new air while strawberry-fans cluster, flutter, you sit naked, your bare feet printing mud. A pair of geese flies over, you can hear their wings wind-whistle, bellies almost touch your longing fingers.

They do not notice your nakedness, nor do the peepers chirping from their secret places, nor the jumble of male green frogs who pile on the large female, she sinks to the pond's bottom weighted down by so much love.

Your dogs startle a painted turtle, her hind-legged digging in a hummock left by some bulldozer. Your sadness as she tumbles underwater to escape, pale oblong moons of eggs that will never shine set among water weed.

It was in that field and forest you found the poetry again, those rubber boots big enough to hold your feet and the bubbling poems like so much frog-spawn. Clouds of bubble with minuscule black eyes.

And the poem of becoming, when tiny legs sprout and the tail falls away. Isn't it amazing how a frog buries itself in November mud, freezes sold and then March sun's sluggish thaw, sings every year.

FROM THE EDITORS: *I was instantly transported far away. The mood, the atmosphere, the visuals, the smells and tastes and sounds. Here is something I can revisit over and over with delight. -TC*

THE BUZZ
by Amanda Trout

A night-walk with cicada song vibrating trees; the very air trembles because somewhere the nine Muses stare through compound eyes like screens, tune their ears to a million gossiping voices like aural television snow. The spies sing musician, poet, artisan, blacksmith, dancer. They sing on a playwright's bronze statue of his eternal meditation. They sing harmony to *Flight of the Bumblebee,* craft bombastic cymbal crashes against a jogger's metronome feet. Some sizzle soft-shelled in a frying pan while their brothers sing of scent like shrimp-fried vegetable rice. Some circle beneath the stars, skip from elm to oak to sweetgum looking for that perfect angle, see scandal, success, savor, strife, sorrow—all the sibilance—until the cicada night-watch dies with their patrons' satisfaction in the artistic brilliance of the world.

Poetry

FROM THE EDITORS: *You can tell when a poem is good by this gauge; if it's not your personal style but you still think it's excellent this means it's crossed any barriers our personal prejudice may possess and arrested us with its sheer ability as a poem. If there is a test for a poem's strength it must be that and in this case the style and subject were not my preference but I came away from reading really impressed with how well this was put together and handled. Now that's a good poem. -CLD*

JUKEBOX
by J.R. Woods

The ring on her finger only slightly bothered me.
I was distracted by her tongue in my mouth
and Freddie Mercury on the dive bar jukebox—
A dollar per play for the Classics;
the Top 40 Bullshit was on at The Basement
and I wouldn't be caught dead among the Greek
fraternity and sorority members writhing in Its depths—
Bottomless American ale with purchase of cheap, ugly glass.
But sometimes, when I was drunk enough,
I could withstand an hour or two sweating
in the rather dense fog of pheromones,
pretending to give a fuck about bullshit philosophies—
The wisdom of ancient sophists
swallowed and regurgitated by shallow minds
whose sole purpose for oration
was to prevail over their pseudointellectual brethren
in often futile attempts to impress intoxicated mates,
ignorant of their infinitesimal position
in the fabric of space and time. Anyway,
her perfume was a relaxing fragrance of Lavender—
abating my anxiety and heightening my arousal.
I thirsted for carnal knowledge
of the divine being ravaging my senses—
sending my collegiate imagination
on an Exploration, in the interest of science (of course)
to the molten core of a celestial goddess;
the adultery not fully registering.
For all I knew it could have been a purity ring—
A gift from her parents which she wore out of habit.
Not some virtuous belief imposed upon her
by the professors of her family's chosen faith.
If I could go back to the moment she spotted me—
The blonde rugby player wearing the ironic T-shirt
and very proficiently knocking back drinks—
I would seize the opportunity to avoid a bitter heartbreak
and attempt to seduce her friend in the bright summer dress.

FROM THE EDITORS: *Everything a poem should be is in this poem; it's beautiful, emotive, subtle, doesn't try too hard, isn't pretentious, is very clever without any pretense and feels 'natural' in the way it's written, as if the writer speaks in poetry. A beautiful piece of work. -CLD*

AFTERMATH
for Scott
by Mose Graves

Word was slow in coming from the Capitol.
Was the fighting over? How many lives were lost?
Had righteousness prevailed, and at what cost?
Did plague afflict the fallen—did it stalk the victor's home?
And when might we once again sleep in our own
beds untroubled until dawn?

The news when it arrived was inconclusive,
so we read into it our own desires
like lovers imagine passion in
a random glance, an accidental touch.
The hopeful celebrated, brimming
with anticipation, while the glum
complained, lading another straw
onto the burden of their disappointments.

Subsequent reports added to our insecurity:
new wars declared even before
the last war's bones were hidden in the earth.

Amid the rumor and confusion
we continued to pursue our daily follies.
We loved our wives and husbands, or did not.
We ate what we craved, more or less. We worked
the fields and haggled over the harvest, always
keeping back the proper portion to appease
our peevish gods.

Strolling by the river, we wrinkled our noses
at the thin smoke rising from the fires
of the refugees.

Only years later did we hear the true story
from the mouths of strangers, in a foreign tongue.

FROM THE EDITORS: *I was struck, as I'm sure you are, turning the page to see such beauty in form. And upon reading, the flow and rhythm, the roiling of emotion answering the question. -TC*

WHAT DOES WATER BECOME?
by Adele Evershed

a sea,
  a waterfall,
    a bay, a stream
          the relieving rush from a once dry tap
              or the yellow-eyed puddles at the bottom of a well
          it is summer rain and the tapping of a walking stick
            the drum beat of a monsoon wedding
        a splash made by a frog in the mind of an old man
      and a new universe found in a rock pool by a child
it is the wakeup call after a boozy night
    or the cooling touch in a fever dream
      it is the new shoot from a forgotten stump
          a silver rush of fish jumping like a rainbow's wish
            the bog thickened with bones of our ancestors or other cattle
                it is a blessing or a forgiveness or a popcorn style curse
              a roiling Saturday night or a tender first cup of tea
          feminine and masculine and the great in-between
      and it can be a drowning or a flood or a rageful God
    tears and spittle
    too much or not enough
    a poisoning and a protest
      the beginning and the end
        and one day
        if we are
          not careful
            it will be a war
          and then
        just a poem
      dripping
    words
      into a
        dead
          sea

36

CASUAL WITNESS

by Tohm Bakelas

picture this: it is early morning,
south of somewhere familiar,
south of somewhere
you call home.

there are power lines
running down dirt roads
where dust never seems
to settle unless it rains.

there are grey birds
flying skyward,
towards destinations
you will never reach.

and you are there,
driving alone in a car,
a casual witness to this
which you'll never
understand...

but you are not there.
you are here with me,
with these words on
this page. and we have
only each other, and
the oncoming autumn.

LENT
by Suzette Bishop

At the fish fry, the priest says he likes
Game meat, will try anything,
Any part of the animal,
Likes bear heart best.
The grief for my mom flows,
The low-carbon emission
Silk-like dress I packed for her funeral tomorrow.

My back to the mirrored wall
In a church basement,
Someone everyone knows
Comes by to sell raffle tickets.
I shake his hand, but he pulls away,
Doesn't look happy.
It's probably too soon after the pandemic
To touch strangers, we aren't used to that,
Or he just doesn't like the look of me,
Thinks I'm too forward.

The priest keeps on telling his stories,
The one about his father, a cop,
Asking a mafia hitman why he gets more
To kill women, is it a reference to their value,
A sign of respect?
No, not that. You can't predict what a woman will do,
A man will follow the same pattern.
Not a woman, she will change her mind,
Go see a friend at the last minute.
Very hard to plan around that.

He gave me the two-handed shake of condolence
When we met, and then chatted
With my sister and brother-in-law
In the car. When he brought up Rome,
I mentioned going there, seeing the church
By the same saint's name as his American church,
Loving seeing the artwork in the cathedrals.
Silence shifted in the car,
My mother's polite smile,
I felt it on me.

The priest later tells my sister I'm hard to read.
I don't want to be here,

I don't want to be in church tomorrow,
I'm not sure my mom wants a mass,
All the people who were at her 90th birthday back again,
Very few she knew, the party more for my sister, she says.
The priest looks disappointed at the turnout.
He isn't hard to read,
While she has that smile in the photo next to her ashes,
The one that means she's not saying what she really thinks.

At the house, I overhear my sister ask her husband,
Why do things keep falling? I think it's <u>*Mom*</u>*.*
I've noticed this, too,
I put my earrings on the bed, and they crash immediately to the floor,
I place travel-size soap on the bathroom sink,
It's batted off, leaves from a begonia drop
As if plucked one-by-one,
A box of Mom's things gets knocked over as I try on her coat.
The number thirteen in most of my flight numbers
Must be one of her jokes from beyond,
Payback for teasing her about being suspicious.
The same flight attendant going out and returning
Who looks like my mom, who helps to track down the snack
I pre-ordered, a comfort.
The pushing and slapping? The de-leafing?
Not jokes. Anger.

My sister says, *Just cremate me and feed me to the whales,*
I'm not sure Mom would agree,
She would say, *Just bury me in a pauper's grave,*
But her ashes are hugged by an expensive floral arrangement,
People are looking at how I'm dressed.
I don't feel her anywhere in the church.

In my head, I search for her at the shore.
Deserted this time of year,
I only see the beached whales,
Thirty so far in just a few months,
Blocked sonar from wind farm construction,
Toxins, or collisions with boats could be to blame.
Why couldn't I stop it?
What to do with the remains,
The huge hearts?

I feel her most as we're driving me to the airport,
Passing the aggie college where she worked in an office,
Cows wandering around on the grounds, she laughs.
A gray, rainy day,
No leaves on the trees, no dairy cows,

My sister prattling on,
Not far from her nursing home, the hospital where she died,
The sum of her adult life along this highway.

But I glimpse her as a young wife
Supporting her husband while he went to college,
Talking and laughing with someone in a campus doorway, tiny,
One place where I think she was happy.
The other, a Pisces dying during the Pisces month,
Even giving birth to her first child under Pisces,
A juvenile playing in shallow waters
Then powering for deeper waves,

Nothing eating her whale heart away.

CROSSING OVER THE MOOSE
by Beth Kanell

It's a funny name for a diner. Newcomers
stare around: the sign says Mooselook,
and maybe the back table will show them one.
Antlers! Long legs! Maybe they even cook

wild harvests here. If deer meat is venison
and pigs become pork, what do you call—
they scan the menu, but there's no sign
of butchered moose at all.

Tentative, uncertain, they work their way
through blue-plate names, special dishes.
The waitress, bright smile, sparkling stud
at the side of her nose, collects wishes

for eggs over easy, a turkey plate with just
a little gravy. Home fries on the side, much
ordered, always piping hot. Pickled beets.
Vermont homestyle with a chef's touch.

Me, I take my usual table, watch the door,
see who's coming in—I have a hunch
that my two friends may be running late
but they're on time for noon lunch.

With a nod to the window, satisfied,
they note the water view, smile:
It's the Moose River out there, wide
as the day's options. Framed in style.

Going home after, I cross the bridge
while at the water's edge a man stands
patient with a fishing rod. I pass; he reels
his line back in, casts, capable hands.

People who haven't lost don't guess
the way old passions stir and swirl below.
There was a man who kept my heart. He died.
I find him in each new crossing. I think he'd know.

TAKE HEART, MY CHILD
by Robert Birkhofer

Drinking coffee just to stay awake
Saying prayers just to stay sane
Saying prayers to you, my love
Just to help you through the night again

Whispering assurances into your ear
They're for me as much as they are for you
Willing these words into facts
Urging these hopes into truths

So take heart, my child, you'll get better
Don't fear, sweet child, you'll get better
Be strong, my child, you'll get better soon
Please get better soon

I know your demons come at night
I can see them, same as you
Haunting, jeering, stealing faith
Raking us with talons cruel

I wish I could take your hurt away
And bear it all upon my shoulder
But I can't, so I'll be here
Waiting, wishing, watching over

So take heart, my child, you'll get better
Don't fear, sweet child, you'll get better
Be strong, my child, you'll get better soon
Please get better soon

I'm free now, Dad, so far away
From any woe or hurt or pain
Yet I am close, so close at hand
Within your heart I will remain

I know you think I've gone too soon
I know you wish I could have stayed
But these decisions are not ours
We'll meet again some bright, warm day

So take heart, Father, for I am better
Don't fear, Father, for I am better
Be strong, Father, for I am better now
I am better now

IT IS SPRING AGAIN AND PERSEPHONE COMPLAINS ABOUT DEMETER

by Nancy Dunlop

Rising from the deep earth,
blinded by the sun, I surface, face first,
with tired arms and a mouthful of dirt.

All winter, all
through the dark months, I have been Queen
of the Underworld. Secure
in my familiar home, reigning over
"the world of the shadowy dead."
My grateful subjects. My citizenry.

But then, Spring.
You, Mother, strike hard now.
You've thrown tantrums to get me back
from what you call the Devil's hold.

You've made the flowering green land
into a place that is icebound, empty of life.

You've demanded temples be built
in your name. It has been whispered
that you, in a rage, set a boy on fire.

And yet, mortals
call you the "Good Goddess."
A good mother, with her longed-for daughter,
Finally returned to her, come Spring.
When I, a full woman, a Queen
must heed the daughter call,
drop my crown and rise
from the blanketed depths,
to stave the havoc you wreak.

Am I, alone, to make all Spring's
beauty? To clean up your mess?
For this, I have
given up my crown,
my husband, my consort, my sex,
the succulence of met desire?

No longer Queen, now
A mere "damsel of spring."
Your virgin daughter.

I am called two-sided girl. Half kore, half grown.
I am called,
"The maiden whose name
may not be spoken."

Mother, you will never know my name. You will
never see me in my full splendor.
You will only see what you
want of me.

I grow so tired
of being needed but not seen.

Is it any wonder I seek and swallow
a pomegranate seed
to return to the place
of dark comfort, where I can be
a total woman, a Queen, fully seen, my name
called out in the velvet night.

Oh, spring, with your warm sun, green woods, buddings and berries,
and laughing flowers:

I choose hell over you.

*** Quotations from Mythology by Edith Hamilton*

TAKING THE LONG WAY BACK
by Michael Shoemaker

I trekked out
in a flurry
beating hot thin dust
on the trail
burdened with
the swiftness
of worry
and pretense.

On the way back
there will be
no such error.

I will take time
to lean on the
old picket fence
and stare at the
far distance of
the mist rising
above the hills
counting my brothers
the quail bolting
the trees
to lie on the
cool damp ground
in the meadow
tasting the tang
of wild raspberries
looking up
saluting the
bottom of daisies
listening to the musical
consonance of bees
that must also breathe
in the sweet smell
of the graciousness of grasses
to sit in playing
light and shadow
almost like a laugh

by the brook
with feet immersed
in cold brisk liquid-
self-transcendence.

You ask me
how to live,
this is how.

THE WEIGHT OF DAYS
by Aaron A Brauer

Eyes that beg and plead,
Like farmers craving rain;
May recognize their need,
but seldom ease their pain.

In days of better luck,
If only luck transpired;
Our hearts were never struck,
By deeds no less inspired.

Though lighter as we were,
And less the weight of days;
Tomorrow was a blur,
Forever just a haze.

Remember if you can,
The night we fell in love;
The kiss where all began,
Beneath the stars above.

But time is such a liar,
That robs us of our will;
His promise stokes the fire,
His ego leaves the bill.

I see in fading light,
The love that love desires;
I fight with all my might,
This end that life requires.

Yet willing as we were,
To call this world our home;
Old yearnings start to stir,
When one goes on alone.

A skyline never moves,
Horizons never budge;
When nothing's left to prove,
Then nothing's left to judge.

The morning sets the pace,
The evening winds the clock;
The sunset ends the race,
Yet steady is the walk.

WINTER
by Tohm Bakelas

Then came winter. Its long shadow
cast a long darkness across colorless
fields, well before it was welcomed.

And the remaining autumn leaves,
those tiny dying fires, still clinging
to this world, became displaced in
crisp bitter wind, danced skyward,
drifting toward some place distant,
some place foreign, where retreating
sunlight refracts the splintered memories
of years gone by in the fractured shards
of broken glass along cold steel tracks.

And the lonely, still lonely, passed
through days like invisible ghosts
without anywhere to call home.

And beneath blue dusk everything
went quiet, everything became still.

And you stood there, a casual witness
to it all, knowing that no matter the
name of the town, no matter how far
you go, you can never outrun yourself,
you can never escape your past.

And despite your best efforts of trying
to convince yourself that there is some
place special, that there is some place else,
you came to understand that every new
beginning eventually ends and that
death will always call your name.

THIRSTY LAKES
by Aaron A Brauer

Shallow is the way I feel;
The bottom of a thirsty lake,
Dry and bare.
Gone is the depth,
Siphoned away
By August and time,
By fate and by air.
Gone is the intrigue
Of murky discovery,
Seeking treasure beneath.

Gone is the exhilaration
Of enticing a lover
(the adventurous sort)
To dive in deep,
then to find (through exploration)
something worthy to keep.
Gone is the thrill in knowing,
There would be no retreat.

Shallow is the way I feel,
Exposing too much.
Backed up against history,
(Now devoid of all mystery)
And fighting incessantly,
The inclination to sink.

BONE BREATHING
by Suzette Bishop

I

Sometimes bone breathing is the only thing
Helping my fibromyalgia pain,
ME/CFS fight or flight response, panic,
Deep breathing,
Envisioning the inside of my bones,
Cleaning my bones, one-by-one.

Something shifts, like helping headaches
By imagining a body of water, each image
Getting smaller and smaller,
The headache getting smaller and smaller,
Muscle loosening its grip,
Calming the autonomic nervous system.

I did that on the couch at eight,
In my fifties I started listening to a man
With a pleasant accent, sounds of waves,
Wind and sand,
                    Not even her bones are found,
I can breathe through my bones,
Send away splinters of pain.

The oncologist's office used to be next to the dermatologist's office
Where I would go, always glad I didn't have to pick *that* door.
Now, his office is expanded into the dermatologist's office,
Taking over, even to the upper floors of the strip mall.
                    A snowbank in New Hampshire
                    The last place she was seen,
                    Her second crash in just a few days.

A few weeks ago, I went in the door,
Some of the same furniture I remember still there,
Empire-style décor, but now a long table
Where patients can sit or around its perimeter,
Against the walls, where I sit,
                    Maura Murray's remains probably hidden
                    In New Hampshire or Vermont,

I don't belong here, just getting checked
For something my sister has, putting me at risk,
That's all, I tell myself.

Some questions to answer about a living will,
Power of attorney, DNR orders,
No, no, no.

I was light and airy, once,
Little weight my bones had to carry,
Small-boned, flexible,
More the part of a poet
Than I am now,
Chronic fatigue crashes making exercise impossible,
Energy saved for long teaching hours,
>   *Something about the woods, snow,*
>   *Gone, being picked up by strangers,*
>   *The small towns like my boyfriend's,*
>   *Everyone knowing he brought his college girlfriend*
>   *home,*
Maybe a little talk with my husband about it almost raining.
But it looks more like I'm just lazy,
Letting myself go,
Not hip,
Monotone,
No more liveliness.
Can I say I've already died?

MM cancer, how I remember it,
My sister didn't make a big deal
Out of having the M protein,
An inactive version of it,
But pieces of my history
Start to fall into this MM place,
The loss of bone density,
>   *Wild Ammonoosuc Road,*
What gave me a sick feeling at the core of my bones,
Disc narrowing and lower back arthritis on x-rays
Epstein Barr Virus being reactivated,
Another risk factor,
The source of my chronic fatigue.

Ocean, huge lake, stream, pond, swimming pool,
Puddle reflecting sky, bath tub, sink, glass of water, pain diminishing,
Me in doctors' waiting rooms, smaller and smaller until
I'm accompanied by my mother or father or both,
Afternoon light diminishing, car sounds diminishing,
A shifting season outside the window,
>   *Looks different in summer, green, heavy trees,*
>   *Is that where she is, a second of screams floating above,*
>   *Absorbed into the tree trunks and leaves?*

Today, Texas summer, but some of fall's rain clouds
After months of drought, temperatures over a 100.
The patients were alive when their bones were scanned,
Living bone, breathing and changing bone,
Ray of light,
What surrounds it simply a veiling shadow,
Lying still in a tube,
Cracks, fractures, lines that shouldn't be there,
Disintegration of what holds everything together.

II

Me and words, I don't seem to want to use them,

It's been happening since I first hesitated using words
As a child,
Not sure what held me back then,
Now, part of it is
Words expected on platforms,
Words expected to entice a following,
Words pretending to adore,
Words trying to dazzle,
Never any stuttering,
Verbs, words in action,
The editor at the health forum
Wanting sick writers to be edgy,
To get more clicks,
To sell more ads.
Action, active verbs don't make sense to me anymore,
Inactive even before the pandemic,
                    A psychic sees her in a river, under a bridge,
Times stuck on the couch,
Unable to read.
Mmmmmmmmmmm.

III

The rejection letter invites me to respond,
The editor mentions sinking for a while,
But getting better,
The reason it's such a late response,
I know he'd like me to write back,
Pick up his words, toss in mine,
But I'm shut down on this, too,
Crossing that boundary never took me anywhere good,
                    So much social media chatter about her,
                    Who might have killed her,
                    Who isn't telling the truth?
The back and forth as if we really care

About discovering another poet friend,
And maybe we can showcase each other's poems.
I've lost those words, too,
A different editor led me on that dance of words,
Into that snare.
Take my poems or leave them,
Don't reject them and expect me to lay down more words,
Open words, a body of words for you,
To help with your cheery-sounding sinking,
        The police seem to cover something up,
        One commits suicide,
Pretending the chipper rejection is ok,
A different kind of cancer or crime.

Cancerous plasma cells gather in the bone marrow,
Crowd out healthy blood cells,
My health history a layering,
Which is the overarching illness?

Another discards my inscribed book at a used bookstore,
I see my words to him, thanking him for helping me,
My warm words, my swirly girlish hand,
Now barely able to hold a pen.

It's insurmountable, transforming words into magic,
Breathing life into words from this place,
        Mystery in her decisions
        To leave school, drive north,
        Not tell anyone,
        Breakdown may have made her vulnerable
        To foul play,
        Left her running at night on a mountain road, alone.

I go months talking to animals, my husband,
Doctors, nurses, no one else,
Taking in words in books, online, too exhausting.

Healthy cells regenerating
More healthy cells,
One typed word leading to another
All I can breathe into you.

IV

        Another girl never found,
        Not far from Maura Murray's disappearance,
        Another abandoned, turned-around car,
        Gray weather.

The energy psychics pick up,
Like the energy animals pick up,
A violent death like a stone
Thrown into a pond makes a ripple,
And the ripple stays there,
The psychic moves from seeing Maura
From the outside to entering her point of view,
A Massachusetts plate, alcohol in the car,
Snow falling on the windshield, into her eyes.

The woods I thought were mine,
Early mornings and sent out to play,
Leaf cover of summer or after school,
Fall reds and yellows iridescent
From sunlight, held in speckled,
Filtered light, birds I couldn't see calling,
Splintery vines, nut-fall, hard-tracing bark.

I'm saying good-bye to those woods,
None of it was mine, the house,
The yard, the woods out back,
Branches swaying in summer,
Leaves swinging one way, clouds the other,
Limbs creaking with snow and ice in winter.

He sees her as a deer,
She even runs almost as fast
This young woman used to woods,
At home there.
She'll see a path and run from him
When she sees him stop and get out of his red truck,
But he's fast, too, and used to woods, snow.

And she, like me, doesn't want to see
What isn't hers,
The moon through the leafless canopy
Telling her she's about to disappear,
Those woods close like a theater curtain.

He writes, "What has me thinking about this now
Is my moment last night,
That moment when I saw an angel
And made her an angel."

Not always in our grasp,
Not always walking in it,
Not always breathing.

SPRING
by Tohm Bakelas

yet again, the season changes.
winter dies, spring is reborn.
worms crawl out for sun.
birds return for seed.
grass grows green.
flowers bloom.
people smile.

the cycle repeats, ad infinitum.

ink on pages lasts longer than
the candle I was born holding—
help me savor things that matter
most before they're gone forever—

the worn maps of memory...
the tired paths once walked...
the changing landscapes of cities...
the greying oceans of dissipating time...

all this, and everything between,
carefully scratched into poems,
will be what remains of me.

I AM THE COLOR BLACK
by Braeden Michaels

I am the color black
wrapped up in a midnight curse
torture dripping down my bleached face
gripping on to the endangered lies
whispers growling in my prejudice ears
sorrow was a door to throw away my beliefs
clutching on to the skeleton chain
tomorrow weeps from my skewed perception
stumbling in the waterfalls, praying to
blurry shadows and the sinister moon
I sip on the poison of a poor man's cup
and I hide in the mist to make me blind
Lord, save me from the lake of screams

I am the color black
severed from the spinning rainbow
buzzards flying around my dying tree
decaying stains, fumbling in the dark
crawling toward the vibrations of the stigma
haunted by my twitching nerves
anxiety and insecurities boiling on the inside
grief jumbled, agony waltzing
carrying heartbreak over my shoulders
I quietly stare into the atoms of my distress
molecules sizzling, bloodstream crying
depths of discomfort, circling headaches
and I seek grace with a pitchfork and knives
Lord, save me from the lake of screams

I am the color black
ripped from the sobbing vermillion sky
distinctively malevolent, serene and ill
tarnished and frozen, inside the frostbite
slightly obscene, smothered in vile
a predator within, carrying a tarantula grin
vertigo parading, obscurity blending
corrosion running down my esophagus
A diabolical mind dipped in scarlet oil
walking with a criminal like scent
cemetery gray with a pinch of graveyard dirt
a night crawler climbing in your memory
spellbinding oblivion, twisted secrets
Lord, save me from the lake of screams

I am the color black
unhinged and sadistic salivating from the burns
scatterbrained, splash of schizophrenia
a thousand microscopic splinters in my cornea
I'm a child of the fifth obsidian scarecrow
untouched apricot skin, labeled as a dead end
hunger promenading, brisk spasms
lightning smacks across my crimson back
fractured, friction is my lifeless mother
I live in an atmosphere of short breaths and
gasping for oxygen among my bothers
consistently sucker punched and jabbed
with crude remarks, self-esteem is hollow
Lord, save me from the lake of screams

I am the color black
characterized as the lustrous sin
specks of halcyon, spots of carmine
symbolizing annihilation and wreckage
disfiguring truth, a heinous sparkle
I strut with apocalyptic and corrupt nerves
veins filled with cynicism and suspicion
doubt trickling, hyperboles drooling nonstop
fiction rolling off my slanderous lips
sugarcoated fabrication stewing
I've shaped my ruthless tombstone
Viciousness is my father's favorite drink
I've learned to slurp vengeance
Lord, save me from the lake of screams

I am the color black
stamped as a disastrous villain
I smirk at tragedy and illuminate within magic
identified as a slithering savage
I slap hope with a monstrous hand
distinguished as liquid monstrosity
I despise faith and lurch in your nightmares
venom is like loose change in my pockets
I've exchanged bitten conversations with
corpses in my slaughterhouse backyard
quietly, I am the joker who plays with satire
and explosive irony, kiss the rage on my cheek
I am the gift you are afraid to open
Lord, save me from the lake of screams.

WATERCOLOR AT 35,000 FEET

by Michael Shoemaker

No snacks
water, no ice.
A child wets a brush
dips in orange
touches paper.
Color spreads fast and wide
an amazing creation.

"Look, Mom, I made a sun."
She gazes.
"I knew you would, sweetheart
—someday."

DEATH VISITS THE HILLS
by Aaron A Brauer

The fiddle moans on stoic breeze;
Death's face coats the barren trees;
Tears that fall on funeral shoes,
Merely rain for graveside muse.

Slowly down sorrow's path
Every living sound is mute;
His pine box rests on braids of jute,
Atop the hewn and desolate hole
Which awaits his final sleep.
Don't be silent mother... weep!

Father waits all these twenty years,
Moss has grown on the stone
Which bears his spotless name;
Yet there is room for two more
Inside this wrought iron frame;
Death awaits outside their door,
But in them, labored breath remains.

Oh great cedars!
Will you whisper their names?
When November northers blow;
The orchard brown and dry
Like the earthen colored sky
Casting shadows down below.

Pray! oh pray, a soul to keep!
For he's been lowered now,
Down into the deep.
The dirt pecks on the pine
One spade full at a time,
Until light is light no more.

Now the path is blown with snow
And springtime seems so far,
Such a distant warmth to find,
I shall sit with them awhile.
Our dear ones left behind.

MELANCHOLY'S SONG
by Michael Shoemaker

It's Friday and drizzling again
while you drive home
listening to the radio with me by your side
and the song comes on.

It's the one that sometimes thrills,
brings moods or something too hard to describe,
but somehow always
matches our souls.

You roll down the window to watch
tiny beads of water bounce off your skin
and just about everything smells as it was before-
something of lavender.

There used to be the taste of the sea breeze
on the tips of our tongues
and the warmth of our hearts
with tenderness and understanding.

You turn into my driveway, stop the engine and look at me.
Tears roll down our cheeks knowing what can no longer be
and what no longer needs to be said.
I get out of the car, shut the door and walk away.
The last note floats skyward beyond our reach.

CARIBOU FAREWELL
by Mose Graves

Downslope from the trailhead
we cross a creek on a
weathered log, splintered at
the root.
The accidents that brought us
here must speak for
themselves, while we in our
tongue-tied boots

stutter up these switchbacks, and at each turn,
just like the bears that grunt
and graze here, gorge on the
mountain's bounty. Even the
burned places feed us: seeing
the fireweed charge

uphill, pink blazing the
vale of charred snags,
refreshes our faith in the
earth that takes what we
love but, out of the sticks
and rags remaining,
patiently, ceaselessly,
makes

new. At the lake at the end of the day,
the wind in the trees sweeps the clouds away.

WHEN THESE THOUGHTS ARISE

by J. R. Woods

When these thoughts arise
my thighs
become a pincushion
under the fingernails
of a masochist

because maybe just maybe if I dig them in deep enough a deity might spring
forth from the gash and relieve me of them permanently...perhaps even by
removing this cursed head from my shoulders altogether in one fell stroke at
the nape of a neck weary from attempting to hold high a head that's been much
too heavy from the moment it was crowned

Screaming
Bloodied and Blinded by ultraviolet rays
shone carelessly down on a gruesome scene
starring a young man thrust unforgivingly
into a light that burns more than it nourishes
and casts unnatural shadows
that are forever grasping
and ravenous
and much too **black**
to possibly be real

but somehow they are...they are...they are very real indeed and the only way to
avoid the Eternal Burn is to retreat so deep into the darkness that my reflection
cannot possibly be seen by even the keenest and most knowing of eyes held
suspended just inches from the surface of the loneliest pool ever conceived...

THIS TREE OF RIPENED FRUIT
by Beth Kanell

I've tried to let my secrets all fly free:
some framed in daily photos of this place
while some are whispered to the apple tree.

It stands beyond the garden's well-tamed space,
bark ridged with growth and age from many years
of witnessing what all of us must face:

our failures and our losses, and true life
which asks for everything—I've heard the call
as mother, grandma, friend, and much-loved wife.

Now apples ripen in this golden fall
while in the house I'm peeling more for pie.
And every time I bake, I share it all:

The cinnamon, the sweet, sometimes the tart—
these apples wake the autumn in my heart.

COFFEE LOVE

by Tess Lecuyer

1
Morning

You cradle mornings,
Smooth out my stuttering day.
Each hot, bitter kiss!

2
The Cup

O Coffee! I reach
For the cup before I have
Poured the damn coffee.

3
Touch

First lip touch, it burns.
If love tasted like coffee,
I would be ashes.

4
Hot Bitter Kisses

Dark as the new moon;
Curl my fingers 'round your heat,
Let you breathe for me.

5
Oh Bean!

Oh my darling bean!
Hot in the press this morning,
Know I smelled Heaven.

6
So Cold

The sun she floats up.
Even cold, you arouse me.
Ice trails down my skin.

7
Drained and Set Aside

Morning grinds to a close.
Where you once filled me, my love,
Fragrant emptiness.

A DOORWAY GUARDED BY TWO CROWS
by Rachael Ikins

Two crows on a beach towel unzip a backpack.
The house rises on its hind legs, flaps its wings,
high on the sugar-rush from beak-dipped Pepsi,
an Oreo grasped with clawed black feet,
two crows on a beach towel.

Later that night we investigated each other
at surf's lip, moon dribbled, scribbled poetry and crows
black-dancing-silver
waves

Your delving fingers like blue-black beaks dripping carbonation,
the scent of lilac in our hair, just us making love on the lounge chair
on the beach where this afternoon, two crows had sipped Pepsi, pecked
Oreo crumbs, and tore into a book poetry
by some obscure Argentine.

One flew off, screaming around the pen in its beak.
Crows are not pessimists, every road-killed squirrel with maggots
every lump of red-ribboned plastic, an opportunity—here, maybe a fox
tore the plastic skin, wads of wrapper strewn, melon rinds,
mysterious bloody bandages
to investigate.

Shiny, so treasured,
a child's neon-pink barrette,
something for a bird or a poet
to covet

Off night's porch, wind carries feathers to the beach,
water licks its lips, rubs sand out of its eyes again and again,
pulling everything on land into its skirts, birds, poets,
for the ocean spewed us all forth.

Delicate layers of silt, laid down with tongues' precision,
strewn shells that fill and spill and fossilize—see, here,
in this rock, impression of a gypsy-bird, wings, outstretched,
bony legs, a tail fanned, suspended amber secrets in the ears of
beach-ponies, their celebration,
drum drumming

I watch my mother listen to the sea, her head cocked like an owl's,
I see the knowing in her yellow eyes, the knowing of what-comes-next.
Death, just an interruption,

a doorway guarded by two crows on the beach,
burping Pepsi, and staggering, drunk on sugar
and chocolate and I wonder
is chocolate poisonous
to birds, too.

THREE DAYS ON THE ROAD
by Vito del Valle

Remember waking up in the back of
> my father's truck
Yellow 1971 Ford pickup with a white camper top
Hearing tires on asphalt
Feeling the hum of the engine
Looking out the window, watching
> Lincoln
> Oklahoma City
> Dallas
> Houston
Pass by as we made our way home
After two and a half months working in the fields of
> Minnesota
> North Dakota
> South Dakota
I'm thirteen years old and missing my friends
> missing my bike
> missing my bed
Waiting to hear the stories of summer pony league baseball
> from the other kids
All my stories are about
> mile long sugar beet rows
> thunderstorms and tornadoes
> buying used cassettes at garage sales
Three days on the road traveling from
> one border to the other
I missed The Valley
I just wanted to be home.

BLACK MISSION FIG
by Diane Funston

You tower over all
Reach up tall
for power
for electricity
in wires above.

You slap a back
with leaves large
as a big man's hands
on tributaries from
main trunk thick
as elephant muscle.

Rising high you reign
Queen Califa
of the garden
other fruit trees
bow below your
ample shadows
like many hands waving
to entitled royalty.

We bow in respect
on day of pruning
remove the suckers
and hangers-on
Search your raiments
with saw and shear
in our steady work
of cracking branches

Take only the necessary
for the promise
more obsidian fruit
come Spring
Black Mission mother
your fruit has blessed mouths
saints and sinners alike
we do not tame you
nor hold you back
the generosity
of long history
Your fertility
from the chalice
to the blade.

NOTHING THE MATTER WITH ME
by Carolyn Donnell

Stop dragging your shirt-sleeves on the ground
and stand up straight and don't slump.
You just stand there like a frump
swinging your arms, not raising them high,
like you're supposed to do.
What's the matter with you?

Why aren't you wearing yellow and red?
This time of the year Oak's colors are bold.
Your brothers and sisters do what they're told,
Why can't you act like the rest of us,
like you're supposed to do?
What's the matter with you?

We shortened your sleeves, but you put them back.
We even tried painting you red and brown
but you're still green, making rustling sounds.
You have to be different from everyone else,
not like you're supposed to do.
What's the matter with you?

Why won't you try to be like us?
Why do you always say you can't?
No one will ever want you like that.
You will never have any friends,
like you're supposed to do.
What's the matter with you?

A woodsman walking the forest one day
spotted the strange looking crop.
Why, he asked, would someone chop
and hack a willow tree like this?
That's not what they're supposed to do.
I'd ask them, what's the matter with you?

A willow? The little tree thought on the words.
Is that what I am? Not an oak?
It's no wonder that I feel choked.

Why didn't anyone tell me before?
That's what they're supposed to do.
Not say, what's the matter with you.

I don't know what a willow tree is.
There are no others like me around.
Where I came from might never be found.
But I can stop trying to be an oak.
That's not what I'm supposed to be.
There is nothing the matter with me.

Fiction

FROM THE EDITORS: *The originality of this piece astounded me. It was incredibly well thought-through and clever in terms of structure, pacing, humor, insight, and compilation. It's very hard to do this with a short piece, it was phenomenally put together. Whether you agree/disagree with the premises there in the raw insight of human nature and the hilarity (and ironically, the truth of it) was potent and memorable. Excellent writing, it would convert a hater of short stories into a fan.* -CLD

START A RELIGION – STAY OUT OF JAIL
by Logan Medland

We decided to start a religion. We picked a day for the first sacrifice and notified the world's media. In the intervening weeks we busied ourselves making robes, devising rituals and creating a dialect for speaking in tongues. We wanted to be as prepared as possible because you only get one chance with the media.

In the end it worked out as well as could be expected. Several news shows carried pictures of my wife preparing to butcher a goat on a homemade black dais, while I sprinkled red water on her head. We danced in our robes and chanted gibberish, our wizard hats shimmering in the setting sun. There was a reaction from animal rights groups which ran the next day, and several protesters showed up at our door waving placards. That night the goats disappeared from our barn, and this too was carried by the media. I was quoted as saying that there was no real moral difference between a sacrifice and an ordinary butchering, except that in the case of the former, the sacrificer and the victim have the sense of being part of a cosmic ceremony. I stressed that all the food would be eaten and the skins used for clothing, and showed them my hand made goat skin robe as proof. After that we were off and running. We went to the market to buy new goats and a stronger padlock for the barn.

Within days people were showing up at our door asking to join. Some came from hundreds of miles away. We accepted their worldly goods in the form of cheques, cash or money orders and sent them to work digging rocks out of the pastures. Holy rocks. In the evenings I taught them the works of the great Zanthus which featured the themes of humility, self-sacrifice and the benefits of hard labour, with special emphasis on poverty. In the mornings, while the others picked rocks and plowed, I wrote the works of the great Zanthus - borrowing freely from *Thus Spake Zarathustra*, *The Lord of the Rings*, and Nostradamus. To give it focus I threw in repeated predictions of an impending apocalypse. We had about six months in my estimation. After study, Shuggar - my wife - led the tribe in a succession of exercises involving stretching, meditation, and lots of deep breathing, designed to induce trance and bring about ecstatic revelations. She had studied Yoga once which came in pretty handy for this.

Initially we were working it as a nature religion. We talked about the earth as our physical mother, and the sun as our symbolic father. When we were fearful, we looked to the moon for answers, and we described our individual souls as the notes in a grand and glorious harmony of the spheres.

Somewhere along the way, a simple business idea got complicated. I'm not sure whether it was the constant focus on inventing a spiritual vocabulary, the hard physical labour, or the evenings of deep breathing, but after weeks of practice we began, one at a time, to fall into a deep trance where we experienced intense and dramatic visions. At first I thought the others were feigning, in their zeal to belong, so I encouraged them and pretended it was the real thing. But then one night it happened to Shuggar, and then to me. My brain began to throb like a blister about to burst open, and I felt myself disappearing into something huge. I had a glimpse of the world as a divine unified force connecting everything: goats humans and plants, and the only apocalypse I saw was what you or I would call everyday human life. It was over in a few seconds, and I awoke on the ground shaking uncontrollably, my face raw from rubbing against the carpet.

The works of Zanthus suddenly took on a new significance. I no longer felt that it was I who was writing them, but that I was divinely inspired: the creator of a magnificent New Testament for all of mankind. We fell into a harmony of hard work, meditation, eating, and study. Once a month we sacrificed a goat under the full moon. After the sacrifice we would run naked through the fields and orchards, singing hymns and beating each other with willow branches. We became our natural selves living beneath the sun and the moon with no concern for anything except our relationship with the great Zanthus, the Animus Mundi whom we felt as a physical presence each time we performed Shuggar's exercises. When we contacted the media to let them know about our progress they weren't interested any more. Spirituality is old news they said. One reporter told me to call back if we were planning a mass suicide. We were disappointed but assumed that sooner or later they'd show some interest in the second coming.

One morning a man from a rival religion came to our door. He told me he was a member of CROC, The Church for the Removal of Obstinate Cults. It was his duty to stop the pagan activities that have been taking place under the cover of our religion. I told him the media had misrepresented us; that we were merely goat farmers with a flair for theatricality. He didn't believe me. The previous night as he lay in a ditch praying he had heard wild cries and seen naked people running through the pastures and orchards beating each other with branches. I assured him that we were simple butchers who threw the occasional party that got out of hand. He didn't believe me. He said that one of our followers had told him that they had donated all of their money to our church. I insisted that we were simple butchers who dabbled in investment banking. *Church* was slang for investment group. He didn't believe me. He claimed he had heard about Zanthus, who was surely none other than the devil in disguise. I countered that the only Zanthus I knew was a back up shortstop for the Mets. He couldn't hit for a hill of beans. The man still didn't believe me. Finally I told him the truth. I admitted that I was in league with the devil, that Zanthus was Sanskrit for Satan and that we were here to overthrow everything that was decent and good, in particular the CROC's and the TUFT's and the SNIPE's because then the world would be ours and ours alone. At last he believed me and reared back pointing at me with a huge bony finger, bellowing something in latin. I grabbed my goat robe from its hook by the door, threw it over my head and advanced on him speaking in tongues. He ran stumbling down the driveway bleating like a frightened lamb. Or maybe a goat.

That night we heard strange wailing in the distance and the rumbling of tractors. In the morning we found that our crops have been sprayed with herbicide or plowed under and that most of the goats had been stolen. For a week we lived on our limited stores praying fervently to Zanthus to make the land fertile again. Nothing grew. We did our exercises faithfully, but no visions came. We had fallen under an evil sky.

One day one of the tribe discovered that a certain weed, when mixed with goat urine and pipe tobacco, caused wild hallucinations. It also worked as an effective appetite suppressant. As we were in need of one we called his discovery a miracle. Each day after we finished our praying, we smoked the *Zanthum* (or Sacrament) and tripped. The dark world behind our eyelids exploded into light and color. Our own births and deaths appeared to us in uncanny detail; and we had visions of past and future events. One night we painted a giant mandala on the wall and filled it with symbolic squiggles describing truth in its ultimate form. I began to rewrite the works of Zanthus based on the new visions, but it was always difficult to remember the next day what had seemed so clear the night before. There was always the hunger too, muddling our thinking. The mandala, magnificent at night, looked messy in the morning. I can still vaguely remember a soggy figure rising out of mud in one corner and descending into mud in the other. I believe it was about genesis and the resurrection.

Although Zanthum suppressed appetite, it never made it completely disappear, and, as the last of our food ran out, the tribe fractured. There was a terrible argument about the final goat, as some members wanted to kill it for food, while the rest of us wanted to keep it alive for milk and the urine necessary for the production of Zanthum. Some felt Zanthum to be a drug and not a religious rite and wanted to return to the old days of rock picking, sacrifices, and meditation. Others simply wanted food and didn't care anymore about believing. There was talk about a refund, about returning to a simple abstemious life.

Within days, a rebellion erupted. David, formerly one of our strongest supporters, announced that he was leaving to start his own religion. This new religion allowed its followers to possess worldly goods. It also forbade the use of Zanthum, tobacco and the eating of goats or goat products. I informed him that he was free to go, however I soon learned that he was planning on taking half the tribe with him, including Shuggar, who had become his lover. The rebels demanded the return of all their money. I reminded them that their *donations* were tied up in stocks that matured two weeks after the apocalypse. They promised legal action and left the rest of us standing forlornly in the driveway.

The religion went downhill quickly after that. Unfortunately I was left with the useless followers - the lame, the sick, the meek. We neglected our meditation and our study and sat smoking Zanthum hour after hour. When we became unbearably hungry, we wandered into town and cadged food and spare change from unfriendly locals. The other half of the tribe, *the lost ones,* found a lawyer to work for them pro bono. He sent threatening letters and I sent stalling letters back. According to their lawyer, the donations were solicited on a tissue of lies - the most obvious being the promise of joy and fulfillment. Additionally, we were contractually obligated to deliver eternal salvation, which we had also failed to honor. It dawned on me one day that this was true: that the apocalypse we promised would never arrive, the mandala was a delusion, and I had failed Shuggar and my followers miserably, both as a man, and as a divinity. I spent the night in our derelict garden smoking Zanthum and trying to forget.

That morning the police arrived. A group of CROCers had videotaped the mandala one night while we were passed out and claimed it was a pentangle. They told the police horrible things about us and someone had scrawled 666 on the barn in bright red letters. There was a swarm of media at our door asking about killings and human sacrifice - even cannibalism - as we were led away. The charges, despite an astounding lack of evidence, were murder, bestiality, incest and butchering without a license. We were innocent of all charges except the butchery. The public clamor was out of control, however, and we were thrown in jail to rot while the cops tried to dig up enough evidence to have us executed. I endured terrible withdrawal symptoms as I came off the Zanthum. Over the months a series of rumors passed through my cell, all of them hinting that my followers (from David and Shuggar to the weak ones) would testify against me. I realized that I didn't want to be crucified.

The date of the apocalypse came and went. Nothing happened. The pain of the Zanthum withdrawal dulled and as my head cleared, I remembered about the investment funds. I cashed them on their maturation date and hired a team of expensive lawyers. At the same time Shuggar overcame her infatuation with the megalomaniacal David, and returned to my side. An enraged David and his last few followers headed for the hills, pursued by the FBI, the CROC, and of course the media.

The lawyers spun a new public image for us both as a loving but misguided pair of idealists and pinned David as the real leader. In a "controversial" verdict we were finally acquitted. We longed for obscurity. Our lawyers advised us to get out of the religion "business" if we wanted any peace. With the last of our money we got a butchering license. We closed our religion and opened an abattoir.

FROM THE EDITORS: *Even those who are not a fan of subjects of this ilk couldn't fail to appreciate the intensity of this quietly composed piece. There's so much in so little, the subtlety and gentleness of how this subject is approached, was heart-warming, intelligent, and empathetic. Incredibly well written like Roald Dahl's short stories, it lingered long after reading, for its sensitivity, emphasis on acceptance of 'difference' and recognition of human nature and the cruelty of judgment. -CLD*

NEVER SEEN OR HEARD FROM AGAIN
by Wren Oldham

1955

Clara and Howard had married young, and they were very much in love, moreso, they thought, than any of their neighbors.

There was Burt, who always complained that his wife never had dinner on the table in time, and Elsie, who always complained that Burt spent far too many nights out for meal planning to feel worthwhile.

There was Madge, who said her husband never took her out dancing anymore, and Lars, who would nudge Howard at poker games to make wry comments about Madge's weight gain.

There was Willard and Jane, and Lucy and Tom, and Jerry and Agnes, and every last one of them seemed to spend far more time complaining about their spouse than they ever did talking to them.

Clara and Howard were not like that. They did not bicker, and when asked about their partners- Clara at the local women's society, and Howard at the office- they had nothing but kind words for each other. On nights that Howard would be out late, he always thought to call, and on these nights Clara was always sure to leave a plate in the oven for him.

When money was tight and they could not afford to go dancing, Clara would put a record on, and they'd dance the night away, just the two of them. They were happy together.

And yet...

And yet, some mornings, as Clara carefully coiffed her hair and applied her lipstick, as she gazed at her own pretty painted face in the vanity mirror, she couldn't help the hollow feeling that overcame her.

Some nights, when it was Howard's turn to host the weekly poker game, Clara would creep down the hall to watch them, all the men in their button-down shirts and their oil-slicked hair, and be possessed of such a terrible longing that she was afraid to put it to words.

Though he never would have admitted it, Howard, too, sometimes wondered what could have been. Whenever Clara held a luncheon for the women's society, he would find himself entranced by her cohorts- with their bright flowing skirts, their lips and nails all painted in red and pink and magenta, Howard couldn't help but feel an ache in his chest, couldn't help but admire their beauty.

But neither could bear the thought of upsetting the other, and so Clara and Howard tried to keep their longings to themselves.

As time went on, though, it only grew more difficult.

Howard would sometimes catch a whiff of perfume from one of the pretty young secretaries at the office, and it would leave his head spinning.

Clara, meanwhile, often caught herself staring at the men who worked the grocery counter, with their strong, broad shoulders and gruff, stubbled faces.

And it built and built and built until one night, Clara stayed out late at a women's society fundraiser.

While Howard gazed at the woman in his bedroom.

She was tall and beautiful, her lips stained bright red, and her nails freshly painted to match. As Howard watched, she danced and twirled, Clara's best skirt fanning around her as she did. Sometimes she paused, posed for him, mouth slightly parted, a come-hither look in her eyes.

This is what Clara came home to that night.

She stood, open-mouthed, in the doorway to the bedroom they shared. She did not speak. Howard's mind raced as he struggled to formulate some lie, some explanation that would paint over this secret with a happy veneer, but he found himself at a loss.

After a moment, Clara stepped away, still silent, and Howard was left alone. They did not speak on the matter, not that night or any of the three nights after.

On the fourth night, Howard's boss needed him to stay late and finish some paperwork.

He arrived home well after night had fallen to find the house dark, though as he stepped through the door, he heard the unmistakable sound of music playing.

He followed the sound, up the stairs, down the hallway, all the way to the bedroom. Clara was standing there.

Howard's suit did not fit her well- the shoulders sagged around Clara's narrow frame, the cuffs of the pants rolled to prevent her from tripping- but to him, she was stunning.

She nodded to the bed, where her best dress was laid out, and Howard understood. That night, they danced the night away, alone in their bedroom with the curtains drawn.

Things were a little easier, after that. Clara and Howard would do all the things they always had- Clara with her shopping and cleaning and volunteering for the women's society, and Howard with his office work and poker nights and the woodworking classes he'd been taking.

On nights they were alone, though, Clara and Howard could finally be themselves. They could draw all the curtains and turn off all the lights and be the husband and wife that they had always been meant to be.

This went on for nearly six months before the trouble started.

The neighbors had always talked about Clara and Howard- how strange it was, the ladies at the women's society said, that the two had no children after five years of marriage. How strange it was, the men at Howard's office said, that he allowed his wife to spend so much time volunteering, when clearly she was meant to be at home.

How strange it was, their neighbors said, that Clara and Howard never have us for dinner anymore. How strange it was, their neighbors said, that they seemed to spend every free evening at home, with all the curtains drawn.

The neighbors' curiosity only grew, until one night, Burt dropped by unannounced to see if Howard would like to go out for drinks. Howard declined, but Burt thought it strange that his skin looked so smooth, his lashes so dark, as he poked his head out the door.

The next night, Madge went over, asking to borrow a cup of sugar from Clara, and thought it strange when she caught a flash of the woman through the cracked door- why, in the darkness of the house, it almost looked like Clara was wearing trousers.

The neighbors kept dropping by, night after night, always with some excuse, always clearly desperate for just a glimpse of what was happening inside.

Clara and Howard were beside themselves with worry. Their time alone made them happy, yes, happier than either thought they had ever been before- but if word got out, neither would be able to show their faces in town, not ever again.

After a time, though, this thought seemed less and less frightening.

One day, as she was doing the dishes, Clara casually brought up a doctor she'd read about in Denmark. The following week, Howard told Clara about a doctor he had heard about from New Zealand.

And somehow, though they did not discuss it further, their decision was made.

Clara began to pack away her favorite possessions- the china canisters she'd inherited from her grandmother; the blue glass serving bowls she'd gotten as a wedding present; the tin soldiers she'd played with when her brothers had outgrown them.

Howard, too, began squirreling things away - his favorite tobacco pipe, a gift from his college roommate; his book of Robert Frost poems, battered and dog-eared as it was; and finally, the bottle of bright red nail polish that he'd snagged from Clara's vanity all those many months ago.

They worked in secret, loading things into the car late at night, when the neighbors would not be looking.

Finally, one day, Howard called the office, telling them he would not be in that day, nor the next. This made him very nervous, but he had always been a good employee, and so his boss did not question him, only told him to feel better soon.

Clara called the women's society and told them that she would not be able to make it to their charity luncheon the next day. This made her very nervous, but the woman on the other end sounded more bored than anything, and why wouldn't she be? It wasn't as though one less housewife would ruin the event.

That night, Clara and Howard put the last of their possessions in the car- Howard's electric shaver and Clara's fine soaps and last of all, their precious record player was loaded in.

Clara sat behind the wheel, and just before she turned the key, she pulled Howard in for a long, slow kiss. And as they pulled apart, they laughed together, each giddy with excitement, a part of them wondering why they had not done this years ago.

And Clara and Howard were never seen or heard from again.

FROM THE EDITORS: *Having hiked and lived for years in the Pacific Northwest, as well as Southeast Alaska, I could immediately picture myself on the trail Michael took. The smells and sounds and feel underfoot. And how I've imagined meeting the same creature he did. I rather enjoyed sharing the tea and hospitality with them both. -TC*

TEA IN THE PACIFIC NORTHWEST
by Jim Landwehr

Michael's forehead perspired as he worked his way up the trail; or at least he thought it was a trail. He wasn't sure he hadn't wandered off and ventured errantly onto a deer trail of some sort. Something told him he might have taken a wrong turn at some point. He checked his phone, but there was no cell reception this deep in the Oregon forest, so it was tough to tell. He decided he'd give it another hundred yards and if it didn't look more promising, he'd retrace his steps to the fork in the path where he thought he might have made the wrong turn.

He lumbered forward scanning deep in the trees immediately ahead, as well as in his periphery. A light mist rained down giving everything a surreal feel and making details that were once clear, fuzzy. Peering into the forest off to his left, he saw a bulge at the base of one of the towering Douglass firs in the distance. He stopped in the middle of the path for a closer look. Like the rest of the trees in the forest, the large aberration was covered in green moss and stuck out like a huge wart on the trunk. From where he stood, it looked tall enough to stand in.

His curiosity got the better of him and he stepped off the trail in the direction of the hut. He picked his way carefully through ground-hugging ferns, stepping over logs and other decay on the forest floor. Depending on what he was approaching, he didn't want to startle whatever it was that lived in this makeshift hut. The hut was covered in lichens and moss with much of the exterior constructed of a combination of pine branches and large chunks of tree bark likely stripped from some of the many fallen trees in the forest. He walked around the structure looking for an entrance and found one on the eastern side of the tree. Whoever it was that built this thing knew enough to put the door on the sheltered side of the weather.

Michael slowly pulled back the pine bough door. He peered in to see a gigantic hairy beast holding a book and staring back at him. The beast had a huge forehead and matted, gnarled hair from head to toe. Off to one side appeared to be a fire pit with extinguished residue from past fires. A few wooden dishes were stacked in a pile adjacent to the fire pit. A pile of small bones from perhaps a rabbit or squirrel sat stripped clean next to it. The hut smelled of sweat, bad breath, and stale smoke. Michael froze in total fear as he and the beast locked gazes for a few awkward seconds.

"Can I help you?" the beast said in perfect English.

Michael raised his eyebrows in surprise.

"Uh, sorry. What the? You can speak?"

"Yes, sir. As can you, apparently," the beast replied. Michael's heart hammered in his chest, ramping up for his flight or fight. He had only seconds to decide whether to make a run for it or stay put and see what happens. It seemed, at least at this first verbal exchange, that this Sasquatch, or whatever this was, was friendly.

"Yeah, I can speak. Um, I guess this might sound strange, but can I come in?"

"Surely. There's a stump for you over there," he said, gesturing to a nearby makeshift seat. "Make yourself at home."

Michael tried to fathom what was happening. The beast sitting on his own stump had to stand at least seven feet tall, judging from the torso and the size of its limbs. Even stranger, he had just set down a tattered copy of Kurt Vonnegut's classic, *Slaughterhouse Five* that he'd been holding prior to Michael's interruption.

"Thank you. You are too kind," Michael responded.

"Is there such a thing as too much kindness?" the beast asked.

"What? I mean, no. I guess not. It's just a saying we have among us humans."

The beast tilted its head as though it didn't understand.

"It's hard to explain," Michael said. "Sometimes we mean well but our phrases end up sounding negative. It's a nuance of the language, you see."

The beast nodded, though did not appear convinced.

"Would you like something to eat? I have dried mushrooms or some fresh lichens."

Michael saw a small pile of mushrooms and other foraged items nested one of the corners.

"No thank you. Can I offer you some trail mix, though? I'm guessing you've never had anything like this. It's a mixture of chocolate, raisins, nuts and dried fruit."

The beast furrowed its brow in apparent interest. "Sounds like something I need to try."

Michael pulled a plastic Ziploc baggie out of his coat pocket and opened it. He reached across and offered some to the beast. The beast reached out with long, weathered fingers and took some from the bag. It looked at the small pile in its palm then picked up a shelled peanut between thumb and forefinger, eyeing it suspiciously."

"Never seen a nut like this."

"Those are peanuts. They grow underground. Try it."

The beast popped the nut into his mouth, chewed, and swallowed it.

"Mmmm...that's quite good."

"Yeah, they're my favorite nut. But hey, try one of the colored candies. They're called M&Ms. The secret is in the center."

Again the beast picked one from his open palm, eyed it, and popped it in its mouth. After chewing it a few seconds, it turned its head and spit the remnants of the candy onto the dirt floor.

"Ackaka! That tastes like dirt! Do you humans really eat these things?"

Michael laughed nervously and nodded his head. "Yes. It's called chocolate and is considered a sweet treat among humans."

"Ackaka! Horrible stuff!"

The beast set the rest of the trail mix on a makeshift table and reached and dipped a wooden cup into a makeshift bucket of water. It took a swig, rinsed its mouth out and spat.

Michael laughed quietly and apologized. "I'm sorry. I thought you'd really like those."

The beast wrinkled his nose and spat again.

"If you don't mind, I have to ask. It might sound a little odd, but you're a Bigfoot, right?"

The beast looked down at his hairy feet, then at Michael, then down at his feet again. "I take that personally, sir."

Michael reeled and tried to reframe the question. "No, no, no. I didn't mean that as a personal attack, but I guess that is a slang term for what we humans call your kind."

The beast again tilted his head as though it didn't understand.

Michael collected his thoughts then smiled warmly to reassure the beast he meant no harm. "Actually, to us humans your species, or your kind, are known as Sasquatch."

"Oocka, oocka, oocka!" The beast slapped its knee and rocked back on its stump, overcome with laughter. It chortled and shook for a full ten seconds in apparent amusement.

"Sasquatch? That's what you call us? That's no better than Bigfoot. Oocka, Oocka!

This was the second show of playfulness from the beast and it made Michael's heart sing. Maybe these creatures had been given a bad rap all along. So far it seemed they were gentler than most humans he'd met. Or at least more polite.

Michael noticed the book sitting on the stump next to the beast. "So, you can really read?"

"Oh, yes, I love a good book. You don't happen to have any with you, do you?"

"Actually I do have a Michael Crichton book, Air Frame, in my pack," he replied. Michael pulled off his pack, dug down and got the book. He handed it to the beast who immediately turned it over and read the back cover.

"Huh. I'm a big Michael Crichton fan, except for Jurassic Park. Everyone knows that dinosaurs could never have happened."

Michael grinned at the irony. Here he was talking to a beast that many thought didn't exist, and the beast thought the same of dinosaurs.

"Well, actually they've discovered many dinosaur remains from millions of years ago. Some would even say that Sasquatches are descendants of cave men that lived during the ages of the dinosaurs. In fact, one of the oldest skeletons found was over 3.6 million years old."

The beast tilted its head to the side in an apparent attempt to understand.

"Ironically enough, they named it Little Foot." Michael said with a grin.

"Oocka, oocka, oocka!" the beast laughed, "You humans are obsessed with foot size,"

"So, how did you learn to read, let alone get a hold of books?" Michael asked.

"Well, the English vocabulary of my parents was passed on to me. From there I took it upon myself to read as much as I could which increased my literacy and grammar significantly. The English language is really pretty simplistic especially for creatures like me considering the size of my brain. I don't mean to brag here but your language is nothing special. For years our community communicated using a complex language of 50,000 grunts, clicks and hand gestures. Since the English language was assimilated, it has sort of dumbed down our culture."

Michael laughed at the comment and his eyes drew again to the size of the beast's head. It was half again larger than an ordinary human head. Even weirder was the sagittal crest running from the top of its forehead to the back of the skull. Was there more brain matter tucked into this narrow ridge? If so, would help explain a lot about the intelligence it was displaying.

Michael shifted on his stump and crossed his leg at the knee. His interest in this beast was keen and intense. His simple hike in the forest was quickly turning into an anthropological interview of an unknown culture and people group. Early in his undergraduate years at the University of Oregon, he'd taken a fair number of anthropology classes and understood the significance of the need to understand, yet not impact, the people being studied.

"So, you said you read as much as you can. Where do you get your books?"

"Mainly from the town landfill. You humans throw away a lot of stuff. But I only go in search of books and magazines. I've only got a few novels on hand, the rest I've loaned out to friends and family. Believe me though, it's tricky getting them at night. To go in broad daylight would be suicide for me. I've read enough novels about your guns and your thirst to kill."

The comment drew a sober look from Michael. Here was a beast previously assumed to be primitive and simple-minded calling out the human race for their inhumanity to one another. The beast had a point and in a small way, it made Michael ashamed to be part of the human race.

"So, tell me, how far back does your history go? How long have you been in this area of North America?"

"While I am sure it goes back thousands of years, however we Malterns are not gifted with keen long-term memories and thus don't have an oral history to draw from. At best, we can remember back thirty days or so. I think this limited ability is both a blessing and a curse. The additional brain space occupied by long-term memory can be used for other, perhaps more important tasks, like identifying which types of dirt are best for making tea."

"Wait. Did you say you make tea from dirt? And did you call yourself Malterns?"

The beast reared back on its stump again, "Oocka, oocka, oocka! You humans have so many questions. You are an inquisitive species aren't you? But, yes, finding soil with the right composition of decayed plants and organic matter is almost a science among us. Travis, my elder cousin Maltern, is what we call a dirt-spotter and has a knack for finding the best tea grounds from, well, from the ground. Oocka, oocka!"

The beast was clearly amused by its own joke. Its laughter made Michael pause again and realize how similar these creatures were to his own species, yet they still had their own unique personalities. If there was one thing he'd never expected from all his past interest and suspicion about their existence, it was that they would have a sense of humor. They seemed gentle enough and this new wrinkle of humor gave him an appreciation for the sophistication of these creatures.

"What do you eat? How do you maintain that Maltern figure?" Michael said with a bit of snark to his voice.

"Oh, we eat a lot of foraged greens, ferns, mosses and the like. It keeps us regular, that's for sure. Oocka, oocka, oocka!" The beast's fur shook from the weight of its laughter.

"But seriously, greens and the occasional rabbit we snare or deer we might take down. Meat is hard to come by, but when it does, we make a point of cooking it with some of the finest fungi we can find.

"I can certainly honor that, though I doubt there are many out there that would believe such a far-fetched story as an actual conversation about food, culture and books with a Sasquatch. Oh, sorry. I mean, Maltern."

"Why is that so far-fetched?"

"Well, I mean, none of us humans ever thought your species could speak, let alone so eloquently. Furthermore, there is a basic assumption that given your size and appearance, if you did exist, you must be a fearsome, aggressive beast."

The Maltern stared forlornly at Michael for an uncomfortably long time. After a few seconds, Michael could see its eyes begin to well up with tears. *Could this thing actually be crying?* He was stunned to think that this big, hairy creature could actually have strong emotions.

"I'm sorry. Was it something I said?" Michael asked.

The beast wiped one eye, then the next, looked Michael in the eye and said, "Why would humans assume that about us based strictly on our appearance? That seems fairly shallow."

"I'm sorry I said that. I guess it's just that humans have been classifying and pigeonholing people that don't look like them for centuries. As you say, it's horribly shallow and in the case of humans, has been the cause of many wars over the years."

"As long as you mention it, I'm reading Slaughterhouse Five as you can see, and I am wondering if the fire storming at Dresden really happened. Could something that horrible actually have happened?" the beast asked.

"I'm afraid so. That and far worse things. There were two atomic bombs dropped that would make Dresden look small. Over 200,000 people were killed with them."

Again, the beast's eyes teared up. He dropped his head into his hands and began sobbing uncontrollably. Michael stood up, walked over and put his arm around the broad, hairy shoulders of the beast. As he held him, he lowered his head onto the shoulder and rested it there in a show of comfort.

Eventually the beast gathered himself and raised his head again.

"I'm sorry I lost control. It's just, we do not know such hatred and violence. I hope you understand how traumatizing it is to think about the death of that many humans in a single event. My brothers and sisters would have a hard time understanding how you could permit it to happen."

The beast's reaction though was a reminder that humans have found new ways and new wars to kill each other since the evolution of man. And to think that an "uncivilized" beast population wouldn't even entertain the idea of any of it. It hit Michael like a ton of bricks.

"I know. I know. All I can do is carry myself and work against the violence and injustices, right?

"I guess so. You see why we remain elusive creatures?"

"I do. I understand much better than when we first met. Hey, I do have to get going. I have many miles to cover yet. But I have enjoyed our meeting. You have taught me much," Michael said.

The beast stood up, "I agree. And you have taught me as well. I would ask that you never mention this encounter to anyone, however. It will mean my entire species will be hunted down in these woods and either wiped out or forced to leave our home lands."

Michael nodded. "Yes. You have my word. This will forever remain our little secret."

"I have decided to keep our encounter to myself, as well. It would only invoke fear among my species."

"I understand. I should be going, then," Michael said.

The beast reached out and hugged him. Michael returned the affection as man and beast shared a moment together.

The beast led Michael out the door and waved as he moved up the trail. As Michael hiked in the drizzle among the low lying ferns and towering Douglass Firs, his thoughts were consumed by his experience with the gentle creature. What struck him most was the heightened sense of emotional sensitivity that seemed to be the modus operandi of the beast. Despite the Maltern's ominous size and imposing presence, he was as gentle as a lamb. In his opinion, most humans could stand to learn a thing or two from this species.

At the same time, he knew he could never tell a soul about what had just happened. No, this legend must continue to stay as a legend.

He reached in his pack, grabbed his water bottle, took a swig from it, and hiked ahead.

HURRICANES IN THE SOUTH
by Logan Medland

There is a problem in our neighborhood. The dead are everywhere. It's not just one or two like it was in the old days, there are dozens, hundreds, like an epidemic. It's a disease with no name, no symptoms, no warning signs, as if a series of graceful and elegant murders have been committed by a killer of the most precise skill - a saintly assassin. The dead look healthy, cheerful, with no cause, apparently, to complain. Whatever the reason it amounts to the same thing. I am more and more on my own.

One by one the bodies pile up around town. They gather in the corner of rooms, they stack up in the bottom of the swimming pools like forgotten inflatable toys that have disobeyed the laws of physics and somehow sunk. I try not to notice but I can't help tripping over one as I leave the house for work in the morning - it's the newspaper boy. There are more lined up for the bus - dead in the fringe of grass near the bus stop. They lie on their sides not quite straight, their suits and skirts muddy from the rain. It has been raining for days, did I mention that? It's been raining and people are dying.

Sometimes I wonder if I'm the only one left. The thought creeps up on me and in a minute I'm shaking with fear. To be the only one left! I'd go mad, I'd have to kill myself, and that would be impossible. Nonetheless it is at this point that the knives in the cupboard seem unaccountably sharp, and the electrical sockets flare open for me. The walls seem capable of falling in and crushing me, they've lost that solid look. Everything has lost its frame. But then I go to work and it seems all right. There is someone alive standing by the water cooler - a data controller or something. A receptionist with a thing around her head greets me with a smile and a comment about the weather as I enter the office. I go to my station and file reports until lunch. Work goes on all around me. People are using the phone the fax, the photocopier.

I work for the weather office compiling weather data. This means I confirm again and again that it has been raining an unprecedented amount, even accounting for variables: it's not my job to speculate on any causes or connections and I don't. Some of my colleagues blame technology, but there are no spaces on the bottom of my forms for personal comments like: "I'm losing my mind in here," or "aidez-moi," you can only write numbers.

The restaurants are still open, and when lunch arrives I manage to find a crowded one that is full of lively people and healthy waitresses and waiters. I don't feel so lonely now. Here in this clean well-lighted place, I can convince myself that it is a long repressed dream that has surfaced. No one is really dead at all, it has been an idle fantasy. The waitresses have hairstyles, their pants are pressed. Surely a society in decline wouldn't press pants, wouldn't style hair. But even from here I can see a pile of corpses stacked outside like firewood. They have swept the restaurant that's all, swept it clean for the moment. They don't want people to think it's the food. I recall now how the band kept playing on the Titanic.

Each day I find another corpse. The maid for instance, and my wife. Both the children, my brother, his clerk, the guy who cleans our swimming pool, and a number of famous television personalities all scattered about the street, dead. The priest from the church I don't go to anymore and almost all my high school friends have died. I'm beginning to wonder why exactly it is that I feel so well, at least on the exterior. Why has it missed me? Am I not worth catching? Unworthy of death? Three days ago the president announced that they were declaring a national state of emergency. The next day he dropped dead. That at least is the rumor. His aides say he's on vacation.

There's been a big storm. Did I mention that? Storms and more people dying. There's only a few of us left at the weather office to record it. The receptionist was found dead yesterday. No one said anything about it, she's still sitting there, we haven't taken her outside, we've been too busy with the data.

Anyway the bodies have washed up everywhere, into the trees, onto the lawns and people's gardens, the fences and rooftops, the factories, the cemeteries, yes even in the cemeteries, the hospitals, the schools, the docks and the museum steps. The swimming pools are full of them and they float around with the current and form patterns like the petals in a flower, or like swimmers in a Busby Berkeley movie. It's all so perfect.

By the end of the week, I'm the only one left alive at work. I still feel perfectly healthy except of course for the despair. It seems futile to go to work but I do. The weather has settled into a monotonous irregular routine. The storms have ended. The only constant is that the sun never quite breaks through and the winds never quite go away.

I decide to stop moving. I decide very firmly that I'm going to wait them out: the bodies and the weather; that no matter what I'm going to wait until something happens

I don't know what, but I'm not leaving until I feel I have to. I haven't seen another living person in days.

I wait for what must be years. Days at least. Minutes or hours, seconds, millenniums. It's a long time anyway, if time is the right word. An elongated moment that stretches and stretches and simply cannot be snipped off. I give up hope; I get up and run around the house in a frenzy. I stick my fingers in an electric socket; I take a knife to my arms. The power seems to be off, the cutlery is dull, the days seem to be getting shorter, then longer again. I don't know the season or the hour. I drift.

One day I detect something. There has been a movement in one of the bodies, a scuttling of legs. At first it is so subtle that I think my eyes have deceived me. But then it is unmistakable. It becomes clear the way an island or a coast must eventually become clear to a shipwrecked and thirst-crazed sailor floating towards land on a splinter of wood - in degrees of believability, and hope rising like the moon over the suburbs. Outside on the sidewalk, in the corners of my apartment, in the silence upstairs, the bodies are moving again. They're stretching their limbs and getting up liked tired and lazy people. One by one they stand and leave the room. They rise from the swimming pools like bubbles, fall out of trees onto their feet landing softly like leaves, gather together into packs, groups, collages, blending the way people never would in real life into a great mass of everybody. I want to get up and go with them, it seems like everyone is going somewhere, like to a football game or something, only now I'm certain I can't move, and that even to try would be the start of unrelenting pain.

I watch as they leave my world with a graceful shrug, I try to move my arm at least to wave to them, but they are gone now over the horizon, disappearing into a blue mist that floats around the edge of the street. I am left to manufacture what dreams I can from what is left to me. Dreams of blue skies and friends. Birds and lovers, sunlight, basements and rain. Even now I find dreaming more and more difficult, more and more irrelevant. The days go by, sky is overcast, winds swirling, hurricanes in the south.

WHEN HOBOES HAVE REASONS
by Loretta Kemsley

Mangy. That's how I felt and how he looked, sitting there beside the road with the hot Mojave sun beating down. He'd been there since morning. I passed him while delivering two yearlings to a Thoroughbred farm in Lone Pine. He hadn't budged an inch since. One of the truck's features wasn't air conditioning -- who could afford it? -- so the windows were down. I rolled to a stop and yelled for him to get in. Agile, he leaped into the back without a sound.

There was water in the empty trailer. I poured some into a bucket and watched. He was ever so polite, lapping at it slowly despite the scorching heat, stopping every few minutes to gaze back at me. Wouldn't let me touch him though, rolling over and cowering. Okay. If those were the rules, I didn't blame him. Those sores were gnarly and painful. I shoved the hay bales around a bit, making room for him right behind the cab. An Aussie, purebred by the look of him, although he was big. "What's your name, huh? Blue? That's what most cowboys call their blue dog.

He watched, wary, silent, willing to go with me simply because there weren't any choices, other than dying of sunburn and thirst. We stopped on the way and bought a bag full of hamburgers, not the best food for a dog, but he didn't complain. When the truck finally stopped beside the barn, he was gone. Just like that. One minute, there; the next, vanished. I was pretty sure he was in the pickup when I pulled into the drive, but there were no guarantees he'd be around by morning. Oh, well, he was better off than before, with water and plenty of cover. I poured a bowlful of dog chow and left him to find it.

I never heard him bark; never saw him, until a few days later when the Quarter mare escaped. My own Australian Shepherds, young as they were, couldn't corral her. I knew it before they started but watched their gallant efforts with a smile. They had the desire, if only I could muster up enough know-how to teach them. Like a flash, he passed them, first heading that old bay biddy, then heeling her, then back at her head, aggravating her until she chased him into the pen. As soon as she was inside, he scooted under the fence. By the time I got the gate latched, he was invisible once more. Penny and Cindy gave no clues, sitting at my heels just as proud as if they had done it themselves. They never looked around, never gave his hiding place away.

It took a bit of time, but I did manage to flush him out. A bit more time and he let me touch him. By then, his coat was growing back, some of the sores healed. I coated the others with medicine, watching them, day by day, until they were gone. Never once did he whimper, never offered to bite. That's the way you do when you've been abused: no use howling, no use fighting back. Things just got worse that way. I tried to be gentle. He tried to endure.

It became a silent understanding. If I needed him, I only had to call. He was there in seconds, making sense out of my hand signals and whistles. One horse or the whole herd, he'd put them where I needed them. He tolerated the pups, letting them make their own mistakes and cleaning up after them. Only once did he bite a horse and then only after it kicked Penny, sending her yowling under the house. She was back before long, still wanting to join in the fun. That horse never kicked again.

Then the sorrel mare came, smart, catty on her feet, true cutting horse material, except she kept throwing herself down. Put a halter on. Down she went. Brushed her. Down she went. She even threw herself backwards over a five foot fence. I called her owner, told him it was a waste of my time and his money. I tied her to the snubbing post while she waited for her trailer ride home. The snubbing post was wrapped in tires and had a couple of inner tubes for tying. She set back, wrenching hard at the halter, her body writhing, in anger or fear or perhaps even madness. The tubes stretched longer and longer, as she struggled backwards. I yelled, but it was futile. She no more listened to me than to the whispers on the wind. As those tubes stretched thinner and thinner, I couldn't bear to look, imagining them snapping and hitting her full in the face.

The danger never crossed her mind, until her hooves hit mud. At first, she just skidded forward. Then, as the tubes regained their strength, she was flung forward like a stone out of a sling shot. Whoomp! She hit the post dead on and dropped. She surely was dying, laying there twitching all over. Blue didn't like me afraid, I guess, because he grabbed her tail and wrung it. She squealed and leaped straight up, landing all a quiver but not wanting to lie down again. She stood quietly, without any more nonsense, until her owner arrived. From the sweating she was doing, he thought I'd given her one last work, but honesty made me tell him she might have a concussion. He allowed as to how he'd take care of it, and they were gone. He'd promised the next stop would be the vet, but I figured the final destination would be an auction house. As the rig disappeared from view, I turned and found Blue, sitting at the top of the hill. I could've sworn he was grinning.

Blue sat next to me on the porch that evening. Jeff was gone. Funny. I hadn't thought about it before. It was either Blue or Jeff, never both. I wondered if he was afraid of all men or just Jeff. Either way, he'd be wise. I carried some bruises of my own from time to time, and they weren't inflicted by horses. Blue seemed to know where my thoughts were going. He snuggled up close and kept me company until headlights hit the driveway. I wondered if he ever heard me cry.

We spent a lot of time together, after that. He'd follow me down to the beach, where I swam the horses each morning. He took to frolicking in the waves, although he refused to chase the driftwood I tossed. We'd watch the surfers and think of happier times. The occasional beach bum wandered by, an attractive sight in more ways than one. It intrigued me how they could be so free. I wondered if I could survive like that.

It was the horses. The reason I stayed, I mean. How could I just leave? They gave me sustenance, kept me going, even on mornings when it was more than the air that was chilly. Jeff left each morning, but I never knew when he'd cruise back by, checking to see if I was alone. Once I'd caught him spying on me on the back trails, as if I would've had a secret tryst amid the nettles and poison ivy. He'd come home with lipstick on his face, and then the wars would begin. Not me. Never me. I never questioned him, not wanting the fight. Guess his cheating wasn't acceptable, even to himself, because he'd jump all over me, accusing me of things he'd done.

Blue was different when that happened. Always silent, he'd be sullen, looking furtive as we worked, licking at my bruises when he got the chance. Many nights we spent in the barn, huddled together for warmth, waiting to hear the roar of the engine as Jeff lurched out of the drive not long after dawn. I loved dawn in the barn, with the horses whickering softly, banging impatiently on the stall doors or rattling their feed buckets. They'd be quieter after I fed, but I could still hear the soft grind of chewing teeth and straw rustling under their hooves as their noses shoved the hay stems out of the way, looking for grain.

It never lasted. The sun would climb higher. Horses, pups, Blue and I would work hard, enjoying ourselves despite the sweat and aching muscles. But nightfall inevitably came, along with the sound of the pickup returning. Everyone tensed up then, hating his taunting stride as he came into the light of the aisle way. Tonight, it was worse than usual. A paint horse had kicked just as Jeff was tacking on a shoe, slicing his cheek with both the hoof's ragged edge and the dangling nail. No doubt it would scar. That wasn't the way to make someone happy, especially someone who loved his mirror as much as Jeff. He wouldn't have hit the gelding, with the owner standing right there. Blue and the pups melted away. I wasn't so lucky. The stalls weren't clean enough. Why wasn't the three year old sold yet? Dinner wasn't on the table.

Our table never did see dinner that night. When Jeff lashed out, I ducked and hid, but Blue attacked, going for boot heels and getting a mouthful of jeans. Blue clung tight while Jeff kicked and staggered, desperately hopping on one foot, no match for the angry gray weight which finally brought him crashing down. Grabbing a nearby halter, Jeff swung wildly but empty air was all he hit. Blue's teeth found Jeff's hand, wringing it hard, and Jeff squealed just like that sorrel mare. Blue dodged free, stopping between Jeff and I, growling and barking. His message was clear. Jeff stood up, wiping blood on his shirt, his eyes filled with hate. I could see him trying to find me in the gloomy recesses. His voice shook with the rage his body didn't dare express. "If that cur isn't gone by morning, I'm gonna shoot him."

We didn't spend the night in the barn. We spent it on the beach, warmed by a beach bum's fire, swiftly learning how to survive on the road. The whiskered gentleman gazed out at the foaming tide and decided he'd been in one place about long enough. He started packing his car, making it clear there was room for us. I knew what was waiting at home, yet I was scared to get in. Blue didn't hesitate.

I thought back to the first time I saw Blue. He'd been brave, running away on his own, despite the heat, despite the desert, trusting to luck and the kindness of a stranger. At least, I wasn't alone. Blue was there, sitting between Whiskers and I, growling out the rules. I'd barely closed the door when we were flying up the coast highway, which ran all the way back to my childhood home. Once there, my brothers would come back for the others I loved. I could only pray the pups and the horses would be all right until then.

THE VENUS INN
by Val Valdez

Olde English inns have a delicate flavor, a puff of musty radiance. They fold themselves into the landscape, grasping at antiquity. They have no conscience, but remind those who stay of past times, of old triumphs, and regrets.

The Venus Inn was no exception. A construction detour brought me to Mildenheath, and spotting the inn through the trees, its docile look begged me to stop; like a silent command. A crack across the weathered sign almost split it in two. Painted in faded white letters, it read, The Venus Inn. Its rusty hinges creaked when it swayed, sounding like a cry.

Ivy crawled up the rough stone walls to the thatched roof and a garden of roses and lilac guarded the entry. A scarred tabby cat slept in the lobby, tail twitching. The innkeeper resembled the ancient mariner, wisps of gray hair floating across his skull and a sloppy shirttail over his huge belly. A web of fine, pink capillary lines peeked through gray and brown whiskers. His bulbous nose hung over his grinning mouth like a light bulb in a whore house. His plastic tag said: Clyde. The faint smell of stout and sweat clung to him.

"How long ye be stayin?" His voice had a lilt of the lower classes. "One night. Then I'm on to London."

He squinted at me from behind the front desk. "Ain't had a Yank in a long, long spell." He nodded at me like I was a side of imported meat.

An uncertain smile toyed with my lips, "I'm looking forward to a restful sleep."

Clyde's smile grew. He handed me an ancient skeleton key, "The room's on the top floor, the best one we got."

Looking around the empty lobby I asked, "How many other guests do you have?" His smile stopped, "You're the only one, mate."

My room was small but comfortable. Wallpaper decorated with gardenias and ivy covered the walls and lace doilies adorned the tables. A faint scent of lavender tickled my nose and mingled with the fresh breeze through the open window. A blue Wedgewood bowl perched on the dresser. An ornate landscape, crammed with wild flowers and nymphs, hung over the bed. There was a small balcony opening on that peaceful view of the Anglia countryside. The window looked across a lush garden, and then a vast lawn, until settling on a wheat field in the golden distance. The forest framed the view with birch, pines, and maples.

But soon, music pounded outside. The crowd was too far to see them. Their dancing feet trampled the grass. The somber trees looked on in the twilight, waiting for something. I had visions of Druids dancing with the drunken revelers. This land clutched at memories of hoary rites, never purged from the soul of the soil. I sat by the window watching and chewing on a half-eaten sandwich from lunch. The music. A line or two from a forgotten ballad drummed away, bringing aromas of memories. Then, as I embraced the roots of reminiscence, the music lurched to a new tune, jarring me to other memories.

They played a line from ABBA, then a verse from Queen, the Beatles, and Garth Brooks. Out the window, I spied them gyrating to their chaotic concert - *The Battle of New Orleans. Grease. Hey Jude. Achy Breaky Heart. Peggy Sue.* One Song barely started before the next trampled upon it. The revelers shouted in the glade, their words loud but incoherent.

Slowly, my memory associated each Song with a past tryst. *The Battle of New Orleans* – I was twelve and Jeff was my best friend. We didn't realize what we were doing, but it felt so good. *Grease* – summer of 1978 and Allen and two gloriously sensual nights. *Hey Jude* – spring break in the dorms in 1970 with Peter: politics and anger swept aside in youthful lust. *Achy Breaky Heart* – Damon outside the skating rink in 1994. *Peggy Sue* – on David's radio our first night in 1987.

So many men. I remember and enjoyed them all. My memories were deep and sensuous. No man lasted more than a few months, some a few hours. Tonight my life seems a disjointed array of memories, music and men, like this erratic concert.

The clock showed eleven. I took two sleeping pills. The concert continued its drunken weave.

Knights in White Satin. The drug weighed on my body, limbs sank into the soft feather mattress. My chest heaved and I inhaled more melodic memories. My mind drifted. *Yesterday Once More.* Leaden weights seemed to press against my temples. *California Dreamin'.* My heartbeat slowed and my breath deepened. *I Got You, Babe.* Time stretched and the light dimmed. *It's My Party.* I hovered between sleep and awake. *American Pie.* Time dragged on my heart and memory washed across my soul. *The First Time Ever I Saw Your Face.* The weight of the past kept me from deflating into sleep. *The Sound of Silence – hello darkness my old friend.*

I awoke to silence. A saturnine darkness shrouded my room. The concert ended. My head ached from the blood that pooled between my scalp and skull. Dry acid filled my mouth. I coughed slimy phlegm. My eyes were sticky and burning. My muscles groaned. I pried my eyes open. The sky darkened my window, and a ruddy flickering glowed from the field. Sleep, even drugged sleep, had abandoned me. I was alone with my memories – so many incomplete memories.

I staggered to the dismal bathroom and washed the stale taste from my mouth. My haggard and worn reflection in the mirror stared back. Too many memories. I splashed water on my features, but the regrets wouldn't wash away. I sighed and held my head in my hands, overwhelmed by reality.

Returning to the room, the ruddy, flickering glow outside drew me to the window. A small fire burned unattended near the edge of the wheat field. A small, dumpy figure in the shadows, dragging a tree limb, limped and stopped, and then limped again, weary with burdens too great. Finally, he arrived at the fire and tossed the branch upon it.

When the flames flared, I recognized Clyde, the ancient innkeeper. The debris of the party covered the lawn and Clyde labored to clean it. His chest heaved and his shoulders slumped. Clyde pulled his shirttail free and swiped his brow. He gazed for a moment at the heavens.

Clyde traipsed across the lawn, gathering trash and tree limbs; throwing them into the blaze. The work energized him. His step grew firmer and his back was no longer stooped. The flames danced high and its glow covered his face. Clyde slipped off his shirt and wiped his face again.

Shock shot through me and tingled out my fingers. Shirtless, his muscles flexed on his flat abdomen where I had earlier seen a beer belly. He turned and retreated to the shadows, gathering more waste.

With each step, he seemed more solid, like his age and his past fueled the fire.

As the blaze brightened, I recognized Clyde was not alone. Others huddled in the shadows, flickering in and out of the gloom. The shimmered glint of eyes, the brush of a hand. These visions riveted me to my window wondering what might happen.

The fire roared. Its glow illuminated the whole lawn. The others passed in and out of vision, hiding in the forest, retreating in the wheat, silhouetted in the darkness. Clyde stood in the field, the fire between him and the inn. He raised his arms above his head over his broad shoulders.

I heard it, the hint of a Song. I couldn't hear the words and the tune eluded me. But Clyde raised his voice in praise to the flames. I strained my ears; if only louder.

Clyde sang, and the shadow figures swayed in rhythm. Their forms became clearer. Men swayed to the Song, their eyes focused on Clyde, listening intently to his voice. I listened to the rise and fall of his chorus, the allure of his cadence, the ghosts of his syllables. I could almost hear it, but not quite.

One of the figures crept forward from shadow to light, crouching, crawling, the figure snaked its way across the grass from the safety of the trees. The lone figure knelt between Clyde and the fire. A soft croon passed his lips. Clyde opened his arms. The figure hesitated, then arose and edged forward, toward his embrace. Startled, I saw that the figure was nude and longing for the passion of his caress. Somehow that lithe form, those supple limbs, possessed a familiarity that tickled my awareness. I peered closely. The face of the man; if only I could see.

Clyde sang and the naked man danced before him and then danced with him. They swayed in an elegant pas de deux, not touching but full of passion. In the Song, in the dance, there floated a mutual delight I longed for but never found. I yearned to dance with them. If my ears could hear. If my eyes could see.

As they danced, the fire flared. The face of Clyde's companion glowed in the darkness and recognition stiffened my heart. Impossible. It was my first lover, Jeff, grown to manhood. Rubbing my blurry eyes, I shook my head and looked again. Why did I forsake him? I can't remember; maybe it was someone new, some forgotten boy who stumbled into me and diverted me. I tried to call Jeff, but paralysis seized my mouth, it wouldn't open. When I tried to stand, my legs collapsed like wet noodles. I crawled to the window, and my silent lips called, "Jeff, I'm here."

Another figure emerged from the shadows. His approach was distant, but the darkness did not hide the yearning in his body. I knew then all the figures were nude men craving to dance to Clyde's Song. It was too faint to hear but still beckoned me, seducing me.

The new figure edged closer, passing in and out of the light. Clyde sang for both, his attention diverted from Jeff to the other, then back. Jeff became more frantic, reaching to touch Clyde, but Clyde slithered away, toward the new figure. When Jeff persisted, then Clyde touched him. His touch was gentle, but there was a glint in his hand and a crimson sear as it crossed Jeff's torso.

The Song pulsed. I could almost sing its rhythms, the rhythms of life and death. Jeff fell to his knees, his hands reaching out to Clyde. Jeff was wounded. Blood gushed from the point of Clyde's touch. The glint was a knife. Jeff, my love. Sing with me. But Jeff faded, dying, his elegant body severed by the cruel brutality of Clyde's touch. The Song played on, relentless, indifferent, and alluring.

Jeff crumbled to dust before the fire, his remains consumed by the crackling flames. He sang no more, but his ashes still danced. They whirled about Clyde and his new partner then settled in a heap. The newcomer's feet trampled upon the dust stomping it into the wheat.

Clyde and the newcomer generated a new Song, similar to but different from the one with Jeff. The newcomer, so lovely, so seductive, so familiar. The dance and Song played on. Though I peered into the gloom, and my vision was imperfect, I was trapped. I could do nothing but listen and watch.

The blade glinted in Clyde's hand once, again. The fire flared and I recognized the newcomer. It was Allen, of summer nights years ago. I knew Clyde would consume and sacrifice Allen, too. The men of my past invaded the night, as Clyde devoured them, one by one, Peter, Damon and David, and so many more. Tonight Clyde and his Song would dispose of the debris of my life. Tears raped my eyes, ripping them open wider to see the path to freedom, to forgiveness. This Song, my Song was cleansing me, making those losses bearable. Tonight was my ending and beginning.

The alarm woke me at 6 A.M. The sheets knotted me in a sweaty tangle. I had a vague recollection of last night's party, and the nightmare forced upon me by this place and forgotten guilt. When I descended the stairs to check out, old Clyde again sat at the desk. He appeared more decrepit than yesterday. He smelled like stale beer, and his clothes were filthy, like he spent the night rolling in dirt and soot.

"Ye're leaving, mate." Clyde stirred himself. "Did ye get that restful sleep?" I shook my head no.

"There's crop circles in the wheat field from last night."

"Crop circles?" I dimly recalled reading something about them once.

"The crops are beaten down in odd patterns. Some say it's ghosts. I think it's dance of the spirits." The word spirits raised my head to lock eyes with him, "What spirits?"

"Mate, spirits is all around, all the time. They follow us." His toothy grin turned into a slight sinister smile.

I picked up my bag and heard Clyde hum a tune. It was unknown but still familiar. Where did I hear it? I started to turn back to ask the title but hesitated, and walked out. I drove through the dilapidated gate passing the forest and wheat field, now glowing in the sunrise as if on fire, and hurried towards the main road. After a few miles, I spotted a farmer plowing in a field. I honked, slowed, and leaned out the window. He stopped the tractor.

"Hello, did you hear about the crop circles last night at the Venus Inn?" I asked. His eyes narrowed and scratched his beard, "That ole place burned up years ago." "Shocked, I said, "But I stayed there last night."

The farmer shook his head sideways, "Not there, mate. The owner started a fire in the field and it got out of control."

My mouth stayed open, then I asked, "What was the owner's name?"

The farmer looked down, thinking, "Clyde. Odd fellow. Some said he believed in spirits and such."

I drove through the dilapidated gate, again. A few moments ago, a huge forest lined the road, but now only a few of the majestic trees stood with burned bark clinging to the trunks. The golden wheat field was a harsh brown and overgrown. Charred stone greeted me in place of the charming inn. I walked through the rubble stepping on something. It was the inn's sign split in two pieces. The name was unreadable unless you knew it.

I fell to my knees, tears, and snot mixed with the burnt dirt. Sobbing, I called their names, Allen, Peter and David and many more. I choked, spitting out love, desire, betrayal, regret, and sorrow.

Suddenly, a breeze caught me, calmed and steadied me. Then like obeying a silent command, I started to hum Clyde's unknown tune, the Song I heard at the Venus Inn.

EAU DE FLAMING RUBBER
by Loretta Kemsley

Vivid. I like that word. Vivid. Boring is certainly not a word my life has much familiarity with. Monday was one of those vivid days.

Our sunlit Los Angeles day started off ordinary enough. I awoke feeling great, finished my morning chores, discussed world events with my cat, took my grandson to school, and returned home in time to grab the phone when (name withheld to protect the guilty) called.

She and I met in elementary school and became inseparable. We worked on Dad's carnival, rode chopped hogs with grubby bikers, showed horses and dogs, had affairs, and traveled together. We married, divorced, and raised our kids together. We prosecuted and persecuted our exes together, for crimes both real and imagined. She's the one I called when a certain dog magazine offered to fly me and a friend to New York City for the dog writer's awards dinner. Over the years, we've been in lots of trouble, had lots of fun and sometimes did both at the same time. There's no one I'd rather get into trouble with if trouble it has to be.

Some people smile compassionately at her son and say the poor boy must have a mental problem. Others say he's a menace. The police are among the latter. He called her from jail, mumbling about buying a fabulous truck parked on a faraway street and only needing a few repairs. Could she drive it to the repair shop for him? We debated the pros and cons of whether he expected her to foot the bill (one more time in three zillion wouldn't hurt, would it?) so he could save storage charges or if she should let it sit until he got out in 400 years or, in yet another successful probation ploy, insincerely apologized to all of humanity. Having no idea why he'd been arrested, we could only guess how long it would be before he could bail the truck out.

Still undecided, we set off to find this new treasure. It was an old Chevy plastered with bumper stickers and dents. One described the truck well: "If anything falls off, please honk." The previous owner must have been a skydiver from Arizona because of the out-of-state plates and the placards from an Arizona skydiving club. Another bumper sticker read: "Remember when sex was safe and skydiving wasn't?" I briefly wondered if the one dead center referred to the previous owner: "Skydivers -- good to the last drop." At least we hoped he was a previous owner, and we weren't picking up a hot truck. Little did we know how hot, but I'm getting ahead of the story.

It was definitely in a tow-away zone, and we figured we ought to move it. It started up and offered to roll, so I followed her. We were climbing a hill on the freeway when I noticed black smoke pouring out of the engine. The clatter and clang drifting back toward me sounded like a blown rod. She pulled over, parked, got in my car and called a tow company. The minutes passed, but the smoke didn't seem to be dissipating. Second, more prudent thoughts encouraged us to back up a little. From our new vantage point, we could see under the truck. Every so often, an ember drifted to the pavement, glowing bright in the shadows. Calling 911 became an attractive thought. We thanked the gods and goddesses the shoulder of the road was very wide, and she'd parked several feet from the local flora. We really didn't want to start a wild fire in the chaparral. Such things are frowned upon around here.

While we waited for the fire department, a laundry truck pulled up, the driver jumped out and began to slay the fire with an extinguisher about the size of a trinket on a charm bracelet. As he bent down and peered under the truck, I divided my attention between the charring hood and the jeans stretched tight across his buns, unable to decide which was hotter.

Fifteen minutes later, the tow truck squealed to a stop. Adonis stepped out, his every move elegant, exquisite, sensuous. He shook his long sun-kissed locks, flexed his amazing biceps, and moaned in dismay. Apparently chariots afire are not discussed in tow truck school. The laundry dude cavalierly tossed his empty extinguisher aside and began an earnest debate with the new arrival on the best way to tow the blazing fiasco.

By then, the wreck was flaming pretty good beneath the undercarriage. After considerable debate, at least a second or two, we decided we should warn our two young gods the gas tank was half full, which gave it an equal chance of feeding the flames via the carburetor (where the fire obviously started) or exploding because of the fumes inside. They proved their true hero status by ignoring us silly old grannies and grabbing the tow truck's fire extinguisher, which was a might bigger but not much, and proceeded to drown the radiator because they were afraid to open the hood. That really helped, of course, and inspired me to back our car up another fifty feet.

Suspecting the fire truck needed to be closer than half a block to put out the fire, I suggested our champions might want to make room by moving their vehicles. Seeing a good opportunity to escape, Adonis disappeared through the rolling smoke as flames began to shoot out from the wheel wells and the front tires exploded. The proprietor of the elfin extinguisher declined to move his truck, which was the closest to the blaze. He simply shrugged his shoulders and grinned; it wasn't his anyway.

A fire truck appeared within the hour, on the wrong side of the freeway going south when it should have been going north. Since the flames were engulfing the cab and the smoke was about thirty feet high, we reckoned the driver realized his error and would turn around at the next off-ramp. He did, but by then there was a traffic jam. It took him forever to convince the lookie-lous he was the real McCoy, and they ought to get out of his way. I wondered if the big red truck meant anything distinctive to those who were either thrilled to see our predicament or were flipping us off for impeding their rush hour trek. Several seemed to be searching for the cameras and movies stars just in case we were filming a new television series (no doubt titled "Dante's Inferno").

Finally the red pumper pulled in front of the skydiver's truck just as the windshield shattered with a loud explosion. Three knights in black uniforms casually got out, finished their lunch and began to don their fire-fighting gear, all in slow motion, but that wasn't alarming since the truck was completely engulfed anyway. Slowly, one sooty layer of yellow rubber after another obscured the taut bodies of these angels. Watching strippers in reverse is not quite as arousing but does have its appeal. We sighed in unison. Such a shame our personal Hades was still blazing. Other conflagrations they could ignite were more alluring.

All four lanes were at a standstill, but the commuters stopped cursing as they choked on the thick, black fumes filling their cars. I remarked to my friend whose name will not appear here that I thought this proved we didn't have to go to Syria to inhale lethal chemicals. Her nostrils flared, and her rib cage began to quiver and shake. Putting a hand over her mouth, she pretended her sniggers were hiccups, a deception I wasn't prepared to leave unchallenged. I mentioned I was glad to see she was following doctor's orders and avoiding stressful situations. Her "hiccups" increased, turning into assorted snorts and woofs as she tried to mask her chortling gone awry. One of the firemen stopped to stare, then nudged his buddy. Fully armored, it was hard to tell, but it sure looked like they were afflicted with giggles too.

They stuck a fire hose under the hood and another through the windshield to quell the fire. Unsure of their billing procedures, she asked if they charged extra for the wash job. I stood up for her rights immediately, demanding they drop all fees unless they were going to wax it too. The youngest one turned to reply but fumbled his hose instead, which didn't help our delirium at all. But his partner sobered us up because he opened the camper shell.

We had previously wondered, seeing as how this truck belonged to her son or his friend, if we might have to duck exploding ammo as the camper burned or if we should stand downwind to take advantage of the fumes if green, leafy contraband was inside. We did neither, simply watching and wondering what was inside until they opened it.

At that point, we decided it might behoove us to make it ultra-clear the smoldering ruin didn't belong to either of us, we had no clue what was inside and, in fact, we were mere passers-by who'd stopped to watch the fireworks. However, they thought we were still clowning around and took exaggerated pains to reassure us nothing dangerous or illegal was inside.

By the time the fire was out, the pavement was charred and crumbling, all of the Chevy insignias had fallen off (perhaps preprogrammed so Chevy wouldn't have to admit it was their vehicle?), and I was planning which parts I could salvage for my pickup. I opined that at least the good tires were on the rear and hadn't exploded. We searched for tools to begin the stripping process but not a one could be found.

The noble officers of the California Highway Patrol were not there yet, and the firemen couldn't leave until they arrived. We settled in for a great time before I realized I was going to be late to pick up my grandson from school. I called my daughter, his aunt, and left a message to expect him on her doorstep in an hour, and kept my fingers crossed that she was there and just didn't pick up the phone because she thought it might be her eternal archrival, aka her sister.

At last three CHP officers arrived, unquestionably mesmerizing in oh, so, tight breeches and motorcycle boots, and inquired why we hadn't called a tow truck. When we explained we'd last seen him heading for the hills at a high rate of speed, they called him direct and uttered words like "coward," "rush hour" and "lynch mob." He apparently groaned again but agreed to reappear, which he did about an hour and a half later.

California law guarantees all damsels in distress on the freeway would only be harassed by the Chippys and no one else until we were rescued by the valiant tow truck men. While we were waiting, we joked with them, which made two of them happy, but one of them shuffled off with a frown. Of course, he was the only one left waiting with us as time stretched on.

Switching to a dumb-blond mode, my anonymous accomplice tried ego massage via occupational patter. "Why can eighteen wheelers smoke up a storm and not get a ticket?" she asked innocently, as if we hadn't just generated enough pollution to choke an entire city.

His eyes narrowed, his lips compressed and his voice sizzled. "You need to learn more about combustion engines and people who cheat the state out of taxes by buying Arizona plates, which is a $1000 fine."

Sensing danger, she tactfully explained it wasn't our truck while I stared at the blackened hulk and mused about our recent education in combustible engines. His deepening scowl told us his desires didn't include the gentle arts of persuasion, so we practiced silence.

Eventually, Adonis reappeared, and the last Chippy vanished. The charbroiled pickup creaked and groaned as its cockeyed wheels wobbled painfully onto the bed of the tow truck. Princely muscles rippling, the reticent chap cleared the still-smoking debris, including chunks of melted pavement, from the shoulder of the freeway and tossed it into the chaparral. Erotic images of undressing firemen danced before me. Unsure whether I should pray for or against rising smoke and burning bushes, I turned back to our tow-truck martyr as he requested our destination. My cohort asked if he knew of any vacant lots. Panic spread across his face as he began to babble about losing his license and other mundane matters.

Lest he flee again, she soothed his fears and gave him the address of the repair shop. "It's late and they're closed, so just park it wherever you can."

At last, we waved goodbye to the truck that may or may not have belonged to her son. I don't think we have to worry about paying for the repairs before he gets out.

My daughter was waiting at the front door as we arrived to pick up my grandson. She paused to inspect our grungy faces and grubby clothes. She sniffed pointedly, apparently allergic to our perfume: *Eau de Flaming Rubber*. "You two will do just about anything to ogle the guys, won't you?"

Now why did that remind me of my mother?

END.

LIST OF CONTRIBUTORS

AARON A BRAUER is an Arkansas hillbilly who works the land by day and often writes with dirty hands. He brings a lifetime love of the natural worlds into his poetry and sometimes longs for the time that has passed.

- -

ADELE EVERSHED was born in Wales. Her prose and poetry have been published in a number of journals, including *Grey Sparrow Journal, Hole in the Heard Review, Tofu Ink, High Shelf, Wales Haiku Journal, Shot Glass Journal,* and *Variety Pack.* Adele has recently been nominated for the Pushcart Prize and Best of the Net for poetry.

- -

AMANDA TROUT is a Kansas poet with a love for sound and form. Her work has been published in *Creation Magazine, Bacopa Literary Review, The Lyric,* and more. She is the former editor of *Cow Creek Review* and current editor of *The Sosland Journal.* Find Amanda on Instagram @atrout2972.

- -

ANGELA TOWNSEND bears witness to mercy for all beings as Development Director as Tabby's Place: a Cat Sanctuary. She has a M.Div. from Princeton Theological Seminary and B.A. from Vassar College. Her work has appeared in *The Amethyst Review, Braided Way, Dappled Things, Fathom Magazine,* and *Young Ravens Literary Review*, among others. Angie has lived with Type 1 diabetes for thirty-three years, laughs with her mother every morning, and loves life dearly.

- -

BETH KANELL lives in northeastern Vermont. The National Federation of Press Women recently tapped one of her Vermont features with a First Place award. Her novels include *This Ardent Flame* and *The Long Shadow* (SPUR Award winner); her short fiction shows up in *Lilith* and elsewhere. Find her memoirs on *Medium*, her reviews at the *New York Journal of Books*, her poems in small well-lit places.

- -

BRAEDEN MICHAELS is a married American author living in beautiful Georgia with his family and his own unique creativity. Within his analytical mind dwell the many passages and corners of the world built by observation, investigative perception, and penetrating rationale. He's been published in several anthologies as well as his own books of poetry, written in the method of Deconstructive Literature, in which he pulls apart nuances within human nature then organizes and restores it in a poetic style. You can read more from him on his website, *braedenmichaels.com.*

- -

CAROLYN DONNELL resumed writing in 2003 when she joined California Writer's Club – South Bay Branch. They honored her in 2018 with the Matthews-Baldwin Award and CWC's Jack London Award in 2019. She currently has two novels, *Deep Colors* and *Blood Will Tell* (under C.S.

Donnell), short stories and poems in various anthologies, and paintings on Fine Art America. *carolyndonnell.wordpress.com*

– –

DIANE FUNSTON has been published in *Synkronicity, Lake Affect Magazine, California Quarterly, Tule Review* and many other poetry journals. She has been Poet-in-Residence for Yuba Sutter Arts and Culture for two years. Her first chapbook *Over the Falls* was published in 2022 by Foothills Publishing.

– –

J.R. WOODS is a Pacific Northwest-based writer of poetry and fiction. His work examines society and human nature through a unique and satirical dark lens. He is of the belief that art is meant to be experienced and felt, not merely observed. While the topics are often quite heavy, he strives to provoke profound thoughts in his readers.

– –

JIM LANDWEHR has four memoirs, *At the Lake, Cretin Boy, Dirty Shirt,* and *The Portland House.* He also has five poetry collections, *Thoughts from a Line at the DMV, Genetically Speaking, On a Road, Written Life,* and *Reciting from Memory.* He lives in Waukesha. For more on his writing visit: *sites.google.com/view/jimlandwehr/home.*

– –

KACI SKILES LAWS is a closet cat-lady and creative writer who reads and writes voraciously in the quiet moments between motherhood and managing Crohn's Disease. She was a 2023 winner for Button Poetry's short form contest, and her short story "Eugene" was nominated for a Pushcart Prize in 2022 by *Dead Skunk Mag.* Her most recent poetry has appeared in *3Elements Review, River Teeth Journal, Blood Tree Literature,* and elsewhere. Her poetry books *Strange Beauty* and *Summer Storms* are available on Amazon, and her most recent chapbook *Smile, Child* is available from Bottlecap Press. She is currently working on a horror collection called *Whose Hand Was I Holding? kaciskileslawswriter.wordpress.com*

– –

KATHRYN O'DAY is pursuing an MFA in Creative Nonfiction at Northwestern University and writing a memoir about her former life as a teacher in Chicago Public Schools. Her interviews and essays have appeared in *Another Chicago Magazine, Pangyrus, TriQuarterly,* and *Prose Online.* Much of her free time is spent wandering around the Cook County Forest Preserve, composing long elaborate lists, and dreaming of the day her book becomes a bestseller.

– –

LOGAN MEDLAND is a Canadian-born musician and writer living in New York. He has performed on Broadway and around the world as a music director for musicals and has written several original musicals, most recently *Love Goddess: the Rita Hayworth Musical,* which played Off-West End in London in 2022.

LORETTA KEMSLEY is a horsewoman and writer who loves to combine her two loves whenever possible.

– –

MICHAEL SHOEMAKER is a poet, writer, and photographer. His book *Rocky Mountain Reflections* will be published by Poets' Choice Publications in November 2023. His writing has appeared in *Ancient Paths Literary Journal, Last Leaves Literary Magazine, Front Porch Review, Littoral Magazine, Clayjar Review, Compass Literary Magazine, The Sunlight Press* and elsewhere. He lives in Magna, Utah with his wife and son where he enjoys looking out on the Great Salt Lake every day. Michael has been accepted as a Writer-in-Resident at the Wolffe Cottage in Fairhope, Alabama and the Tilikum Christian Writer-in-Resident in Newberg, Oregon in 2024.

– –

MOSE GRAVES has worked over the years as a goldsmith, a gravedigger, a flagman, an engineer, and a college teacher. His poetry has recently appeared in *Arc30, Windward Review, Chiron Review, Consilience*, and *Canary* (a Literary Journal of the Environmental Crisis).

– –

NANCY DUNLOP is a poet and essayist whose chapbook *Hospital Poems* (Indie Blu(e), 2022) explores the realities once faces as a patient in a mental hospital. A finalist in the AWP Intro Journal Awards, Dunlop has been published in a number of print and digital journals including *Swank, Truck, Green Kill Broadsheet, The Little Magazine, Writing on the Edge, 13th Moon, Writers Resist: The Anthology,* and *Through the Looking Glass: Reflections on Madness and Chaos Within*. Her work has also been heard on NPR. She received her PhD in English from UAlbany SUNY, where she taught for twenty-five years. She resides in Upstate New York with her husband and two cats.

– –

RACHAEL IKINS is a 2016/18 Pushcart, 2013/18 CNY Book Award, 2018 Independent Book Award winner, and 2019 Vinnie Ream & Faulkner poetry finalist. 2021 Best of the Net nominee. Author/illustrator of nine books in multiple genres. Her writing and artwork has appeared in journals world-wide from India, UK, Japan, Canada, and the US.

– –

ROBERT BIRKHOFER is a wanderer and a pilgrim on life's ever-changing road. He appreciates early mornings, fresh coffee, and good stories. Robert lives in Arizona with his wife Allison and their cat Mushoo.

– –

SUZETTE BISHOP has published three poetry books and two chapbooks, including her most recent, *Jaguar's Book of the Dead*. Her writing has appeared in many journals and anthologies and received an Honorable Mention in the Pen 2 Paper Contest from the Coalition of Texans with Disabilities. She lives in Laredo, Texas with her partner and two cats.

TESS LECUYER lives in Albany, New York and has been writing and reading poetry at various readings and open mics since the mid-1980s. She is a Formalist who likes to break the rules and knows poetry is as much breath and sound in the air as it is ink.

- -

TOHM BAKELAS is a social worker in a psychiatric hospital. He was born in New Jersey, resides there, and will die there. His latest collection of poetry titled *Cleaning the Gutters of Hell* (2023) is available through Zeitgeist Press.

- -

TULIP CHOWDHURY is a long-time educator and writer. She has authored multiple books, including *Visible, Invisible and Beyond; Soul Inside Out,* and a collection of poetry titled *Red, Blue, and Purple.* The books are available on Amazon, Kindle, and Barnes & Noble. Tulip currently resides in Massachusetts. Facebook: @tulipchowdhury11

- -

VAL VALDEZ is a writer of plays, screenplays, and short stories of all genres. Currently Val is fulfilling a life-long desire to study physics, biology, and chemistry and recently returned to playing piano to compose scores for musicals.

- -

VITO DEL VALLE is a Chicano writer/musician from Donna, Texas. Vito's work has appeared in *Boundless Anthology 2022, Boundless Anthology 2023,* South Texas College – *The Writer's Block,* and *Interstice.*

- -

WREN OLDHAM is an autistic gender-fluid poet. A freelance ghostwriter by trade, they previously had a poem featured in the online publication *The Creative Zine,* as well as being a finalist in Globe Soup's 7-Day Story Writing Challenge. Their hobbies include reading and sculpting, and they currently reside in Colorado Springs, Colorado with their cat and their partner.

www.ingramcontent.com/pod-product-compliance
Lightning Source LLC
Chambersburg PA
CBHW080841250626
47161CB00009B/3147